BLOOD FROM THE MUMMY'S TOMB

Retold by Derek Allen

Based on THE JEWEL OF SEVEN STARS
by Bram Stoker

General Editor: John Halkin

BARRON'S

New York

Also available in the
Fleshcreeper series

FRANKENSTEIN
THE VAMPYRE
FANGS OF THE WEREWOLF
DR. JEKYLL AND MR. HYDE

First edition for the United States and the Philippines
published 1988 by Barron's Educational Series, Inc.

Copyright © Century Hutchinson Ltd 1986

First published 1986 by Hutchinson Children's Books, an
imprint of Century Hutchinson Ltd, London, England.

All inquiries should be addressed to:
Barron's Educational Series, Inc.
250 Wireless Boulevard
Hauppauge, New York 11788

Library of Congress Catalog Card No. 88-14629

International Standard Book No. 0-8120-4074-0

Library of Congress Cataloging-in-Publication Data
Allen, Derek.
    Blood from the mummy's tomb / retold by Derek Allen. —1st ed.
    p.   cm.—(Fleshcreepers)
    "Based on The jewel of seven stars by Bram Stoker."
    Summary: A sorceress-queen who died 2400 years ago
takes possession of an Egyptologist's daughter, despite the
efforts of the young man who loves her.
    ISBN 0-8120-4074-0
    [1. Mummies—Fiction. 2. Horror stories.] I. Stoker,
Bram, 1847-1912. The jewel of seven stars. II. Title. III.
Series.
PZ7.A4253B1 1988   88-14629
[Fic]—dc 19   CIP
                                            AC

PRINTED IN THE UNITED STATES OF AMERICA

890 5500 987654321

CONTENTS

About this Book

The mysteries of the ancient Egyptian pyramids and desert tombs have long fascinated humankind. In them were found the embalmed bodies of pharaohs, queens, princes, and princesses which had hardly changed even thousands of years after they had died. To help them in the afterworld many rich objects were buried with them, some with ritualistic or magical significance.

The early Egyptians not only believed in the survival of the soul after death; they were also highly skilled in magic. It was no wonder that Bram Stoker became intrigued with the secrets of these ancient tombs. Archaeologists were already breaking into the tombs to bring their contents back to museums all over Europe, including the British Museum, but what price would they have to pay for disturbing the dead?

Was there really a "curse of the Pharaohs" as some people claimed? Many fleshcreeping stories were already told about it.

And what would happen if anyone tried to dabble in ancient Egyptian magic for himself?

Around these questions Bram Stoker spun his story. He was already famous as the author of *Dracula*. In his later book *The Jewel of Seven Stars* (now published as *Blood from the Mummy's Tomb*) the magical forces of old Egypt reach across the centuries and once more strike terror into the hearts of all who encounter them.

John Halkin

But first on earth, as vampires sent,
Thy corse shall from the tomb be rent,
Then ghastly haunt thy native place
And suck the blood of all thy race.
                    Lord Byron, *The Giaour*

ONE
The Dream

Suddenly a harsh grating sound echoed around the small, dusty chamber. In a blind panic I turned, only to see the large stone door closing behind me. I stumbled over the loose debris which now cluttered the floor of the tomb, but it was too late. As I reached it, the door slammed shut.

In desperation I searched for the smallest crack or crevice so that my fingernails might get a grip and wrench the slab of stone open. But there was none. Not even the blade of a knife could be inserted into the gap between the door and the walls of this underground tomb. A tomb that had remained free from the prying eyes of man for almost four thousand years—until today when I had chosen to violate its ancient privacy.

It was pitch black now. Not even the faintest glimmer of light could penetrate from the white-hot desert above.

Breathing heavily, I pressed my face against the highly polished surface of the marble-lined walls. Sweat was running down inside my shirt, yet at the same time I could not stop myself from shivering. At first I thought this must be a result of the fear welling up inside me at the prospect of being enclosed for ever in this dungeon of death.

But gradually I realized that a slight breeze had sprung up within the tomb, barely noticeable at first but growing stronger by the second. It seemed impossible, but it was happening.

I turned my back to the wall and stared into the inky darkness. Some fifteen feet in front of me I imagined I could still see the outline of the Evil Queen's sarcophagus, that great carved stone coffin that had been the final resting place for her mummified body. Was it my crazed imagination, or was there a figure standing behind it?

I tried to get a grip on myself. I told myself that there was no one there. That there could be no one there. That I was the first living creature to enter that place since the day the burial party itself had left, leaving behind only the royal corpse and a selection of gifts for her use in the afterlife.

Yet wherever I looked it seemed there were other figures.

By now the breeze had grown strong enough to whip up the sand and dust, which had lain undisturbed for so many tens of centuries, against the bare skin of my cheeks and forehead. It stung painfully, and I was forced to put my arm across my face in an attempt to shield my eyes and nose.

But it was no use. The dust was everywhere. Filling my mouth. Spilling down into my lungs as I gasped for breath. I dropped into a crouch, burying my head in my arms. Then, just as the wind had started—without warning—so it dropped. And finally died away.

For a few seconds there was total silence. Then it began—a low-pitched hum—coming and going but growing stronger each time it returned.

I opened my eyes and lifted my head. To my surprise a number of lights were now glowing dimly along the far wall of the tomb. Seven lights in a pattern that seemed strangely familiar. Yet for the moment I could not remember where I had seen it before.

Briefly the lights flared and the chamber was filled with an intense white glare. I could see now that the yellow stone sarcophagus remained unchanged. There was no figure there, or anywhere else in the tomb. With a sense of relief I stepped forward to look more closely at the strange hieroglyphics that were painted along the side of the coffin. In the near daylight brightness that now engulfed it, these markings stood out with the same vividness they must have shown on the day they were first applied.

One by one the lights began to flicker and die, and yet the tomb was still light. Somehow the brilliance of the painted figures remained. I reached out to touch them, but as I did so the whole of the sarcophagus began to glow and pulsate.

As though it was coming to life.

Beating—like the heart of a living, breathing being.

I stepped back toward the door, but my foot caught on a loose stone and I fell headlong to the floor. The impact of the fall jolted the breath from my body, and for a few seconds I lay gasping, quite oblivious of the bright orange glow now filling the tomb.

Gradually the humming sound had been increasing in pitch, so that by now it was a piercing, mind-numbing shriek.

Then, quite suddenly, it stopped, to be replaced by an unearthly wailing.

I lifted myself onto one arm and looked up. Above

me the lid of the great stone sarcophagus was rising into the air. Inch by inch it rose until it hovered a full arm's length clear of its resting-place. Smoke was now pouring out from the inside: a dense white smoke that unfurled over the edges and dropped down toward the floor, coiling itself around my legs like some great snake.

I pushed myself backward, slipping and sliding toward the edge of the chamber, but there was no escaping the thick, acrid smoke. It was in my eyes, stinging till the tears ran down my cheeks. It was in my nose . . . in my mouth . . . forcing its way down into the very depths of my gasping lungs.

Coughing and retching, I dragged myself to my feet and looked across to the sarcophagus. Smoke still poured from it, but gradually its color was changing. First pink, then red, then crimson. A deep rich crimson the color of blood.

Again the smoke caught the back of my throat and I found myself bent double, totally unable to control my breathing. It felt as though the inside of my chest was burning outwards through my ribs. I knew that unless I could fill my lungs with clean, fresh air I would soon pass out through lack of oxygen. I had to get out of that burial chamber. But how?

In desperation I turned and hammered at the door. Beating my fists against it, striking it, kicking it with my feet, to no avail. It was as solid and unyielding as a castle's ramparts. With a cry of despair I turned again to search the walls of the tomb for some other way out.

It was then that I saw the hand.

At first it was partly hidden by the smoke wreathing up from inside the coffin. I thought that my bloodshot, burning eyes must be playing tricks on me. But as the smoke cleared I saw—wrapping themselves over the edge of the sarcophagus—the clawing fingers of the mummy coming alive again.

I opened my mouth to scream, but no sound would come from it. I tried to beat again on the stone door, in the vain hope that someone on the outside might hear me and come to my aid, but my arms moved slowly, as though bound by invisible chains.

Yet, in spite of this, as my fists touched the door a huge booming echoed 'round and 'round the tomb as though a battering ram was driving into the thick, immovable stone. Again and again the crashing sound echoed around my mind until my head reeled with the vibrations of it. Spinning. Echoing. Whirling. 'Round and 'round.

Until everything went black.

* * *

When my eyes flickered open again, I found myself looking up at the cracked and yellowing ceiling of my Jermyn Street room. In a panic I sat up and looked around. With amazement I realized that there was no reason to be afraid. The horror of the mummy's tomb had been nothing more than a nightmare, a dreadful dream that had seemed more real, more vivid, than life itself.

With a sigh of relief I slumped back against the pillows and let my eyes close, hoping to return to a more restful sleep, but immediately the sound of banging began again—more distant this time.

In one move I threw off the covers and swung my legs around to sit on the edge of the bed. Someone was hammering at the door.

I looked across at the clock on the far wall. I could just make out the fingers pointing to a few minutes after four in the morning.

Still the banging continued—a regular, insistent knocking—though no one was making any attempt to answer it. Usually the housekeeper answered the door no matter what time of day or night anyone called, yet it seemed that in this instance she had no intention of doing so.

Annoyed, I put on my slippers and picked up a bathrobe, pulling it on as I descended the four flights of stairs that took me down to street level.

"All right, all right, I'm coming," I called out, as I turned the key in the lock and pulled back the heavy bolts.

Swinging the door open, I looked out. On the step stood a tall groom. He was smartly dressed and wore riding boots that gleamed even in the feeble light of the street lamp. As our eyes met he took off his hat and bowed his head slightly.

"Begging your pardon, sir, and sorry to be disturbing you at this time of night, but I was given strictest instructions to knock until someone answered the door. No matter how long it took. It's a matter of the greatest importance, sir."

Irritated, I waved away his apologies.

"Please get to the point. What is it you want?"

The groom glanced over his shoulder as though making sure that there was no one else within earshot to hear his business. Then, dropping his voice to a whisper, he said: "Not 'what' I want, sir. Who. I'm looking for Mr. Malcolm Ross. A young lawyer, so I'm led to believe. He does live here, doesn't he, sir? This is the address I was given."

I was less certain of myself now. I looked across the street. In the dim light of the gas lamp opposite stood a horse and carriage. The driver was clearly watching the progress of our conversation. Slowly my eyes returned to the groom, and I answered, "I am Malcolm Ross. What do you want with me?"

The man's hand went immediately to his coat pocket, and he pulled out a letter that he passed to me.

"If you are Mr. Ross, sir, this letter is for you."

I turned the envelope to the light of the street lamp. On it were written the words "Malcolm Ross Esquire" in handwriting that I did not recognize as belonging to any of my friends or relatives.

"Very well," I said. "You've delivered the letter. Is there something else?"

Again the uneasy glance over the shoulder before replying.

"Beg your pardon, sir, but I was expressly told that you were to read the letter straight away. And that I was to wait for you to get ready. So that you could return with me now, sir." He nodded toward the carriage. "The carriage is waiting, sir."

"And what if I have no wish to return with you?"

The man looked uncomfortable, but merely shrugged his shoulders.

I tore open the envelope and removed the note. Again no address. No date, no formalities. Just a few hurriedly scrawled sentences.

"Come at once. Something terrible has happened. I think I may be in great danger. Please hurry. It is a matter of life and death. Margaret Trelawney."

TWO
The Crime

Some ten minutes later I had returned to my room, dressed, and was making my way back to the waiting carriage. As I crossed the road a suspicious policeman stepped forward from the shadows.

"Something wrong, sir?" he asked. "Anything I can do?"

I shook my head and thanked him for his trouble, but did not dare stop and explain why I was rushing away at that hour of the night. Not only was I reluctant to waste a single moment, but as yet I had no idea whether the police had been informed of Miss Trelawney's trouble.

The instant I was seated in the carriage the driver cracked the whip and we were off. The wheels rattled over the cobbled streets as we turned out of Jermyn Street and into Piccadilly.

It was market morning, and already carts loaded with fruits and vegetables were streaming in from the countryside. I noted that we were heading west.

I turned to the groom.

"Do you have any idea why Miss Trelawney wishes to see me so urgently?" I tried to make my voice sound calm, even though inside my heart was beating fit to burst.

"Only that the butler woke me up about half-past

three, sir, and said I was to get the carriage ready urgently to fetch the doctor."

"The doctor?"

"Yes sir."

"So before you came for me you took a doctor to the house?"

The groom shook his head. "No sir, begging your pardon, sir. Before we could get the horses out of the stables and hitched up tothe carriage, Miss Trelawney herself came and said Thomas the footman had run to tell the doctor instead, sir, on account of the doctor has his own carriage. Then she gave me the letter and told Morgan the coachman and me to get over to your address, sir, and to do everything we could to persuade you to return with us."

"And that's all you know?"

The groom nodded.

"But you think that the doctor was not being called to attend to Miss Trelawney herself?" I was worried now that Margaret might have suffered some injury or illness.

"I don't think so, sir," the groom replied. "Or what would she be doing outside giving us our orders? Mind, I did notice that on her hands there was . . ."

Here he stopped and sat back in his seat, obviously feeling that what he had been about to say would be better left unsaid.

"Go on," I said gently.

"I think I've said too much already, sir," he whispered. "I think I better hold my tongue now, or I might say something I will later regret."

There was plainly something worrying the man, and for a moment I said nothing, not wishing to push him into betraying something his conscience told him to

11

keep silent about. But I knew that if I was to be of any help in this situation—whatever it might be—I simply had to find out as much as I could about what had already happened.

I decided to try and reason with him.

"Look," I said calmly but firmly. "I understand that you have a natural desire not to say anything you think Miss Trelawney might not wish you to mention. But she has sent for me to help her with the problems she is facing. Does that not indicate that she has nothing to hide from me!"

For a few seconds the groom considered my words. Then, having apparently decided that there must be some truth in them, he took his courage in both hands and replied, "I think you must be right, sir. So I'll tell you what I know. The fact is, when Miss Trelawney came out to give us the letter I brought to you, her hands were stained with blood."

"Blood?" I gasped. "Are you sure?"

The man shrugged and made a slight turn of the head.

"It was dark, sir. There's no denying that. But she stepped into the hall for a moment, where it was light, so that I might read the address she had written on a piece of paper. It was then that I saw the brown-red staining on her hands. Also on the hem of her gown, sir, and on her slippers."

I tried to hide my feelings of horror and fear. But the groom was no fool. He immediately realized that his words had had a deep effect on me. In an effort to calm my fears he spoke again.

"I could be wrong, sir. I may well be wrong."

"Yes, of course." I leaned back in my seat to indicate

that the conversation was at an end. I desperately needed time to think.

It was difficult to believe now, but I had first met Miss Trelawney only two days before. I had been visiting the house of a colleague, another penniless young lawyer struggling to make his way in the world of the law courts, and his mother had kindly asked me to join them for afternoon tea. Being reluctant in my current hard-pressed state to refuse any offer of food and drink, I readily accepted her invitation. As luck would have it, Margaret Trelawney was visiting my friend's younger sister, and so we came to be introduced.

I was at once struck by her unusual beauty. She was dark, almost raven-haired, with a slightly olive skin, exaggerated I thought by the effects of the recent fine summer weather. This coloring suggested the possibility of a Mediterranean background. And yet her eyes were the clearest, most piercing blue I had ever seen.

We talked for a little while, and she mentioned that the next day she was intending to visit the British Museum to look at its fine Egyptian collection.

I had to admit that I was sadly ignorant of such things. But not wanting to miss the chance of seeing her again, I said that I had also been thinking of paying the Museum a visit. Unfortunately, the next morning I was due in court to defend a young man from Southwark on a charge of housebreaking, so it seemed that our chances of making the visit together were remote.

However, the next morning, when I arrived at the courts, I was called down to the cells and told that my client had decided to plead guilty—probably because he thought that with me defending him he had little or no chance of winning the case anyway.

The poor fellow was sent off to prison, leaving me with plenty of time to go in search of Miss Trelawney at the Museum.

After much searching among the statues and relics of ancient Egypt, I found her examining the mummified body of a cat.

She seemed fascinated by it, apparently because— she told me later—her father had a very similar example in his room. I pretended to share her interest, though in reality the thought of that three-thousand-year-old cat wrapped inside those bandages made me feel distinctly ill.

Eventually, after examining several dozen other mummified exhibits, I suggested that we might have tea together.

To my relief she agreed. The rest of the afternoon was most enjoyable. For a couple of hours we sat and talked happily over tea and pastries, and then took a gentle walk in the sunshine around the busy squares of Bloomsbury. Finally I saw her into a hansom cab and left her with the hope in my heart that some day we might meet again.

Now, less than twelve hours later, I had been awakened from my bed in the middle of the night, summoned by a mysterious note to a strange house, and told that Miss Trelawney herself appeared to be covered with blood. It really was an extraordinary sequence of events.

Suddenly my thoughts were brought back to the present with a jolt as the carriage shuddered to a halt. We had pulled up outside a large house set back from the road in its own grounds and surrounded by a high brick wall topped with spiked iron railings. It was not an attractive house, and in the gray light of dawn appeared to have little to recommend it.

The groom had jumped from the carriage the moment the horses had drawn to a standstill and had run across to ring a bell on one of the gateposts. While he waited for someone to respond he came back to the carriage.

"I'd be much obliged, sir, if you would not mention to Miss Trelawney the things I said to you on the journey here," he said nervously. "I wouldn't want her to think I'd been speaking out of turn, sir."

"Of course not," I agreed. "I have no intention of saying anything that will embarrass you. You have been most helpful. And I know that you only have your mistress's interests at heart."

The groom nodded and returned to the gate. Another servant had arrived by now, and the two men had a brief conversation. The gatekeeper then looked toward the carriage and shrugged his shoulders, removed a large bunch of keys from the pocket of his overcoat, and proceeded to unlock the padlock and draw back the heavy bolts. He dragged open the gates just wide enough for the carriage to pass through. The coachman flicked his whip and the horses trotted forward.

As we passed the gatekeeper I had an uneasy feeling that I had seen him somewhere before, though for the life of me I could not think where.

A moment later the carriage had drawn up in front of the main entrance to the house. The groom opened the carriage door and gave me his hand to help me down.

Without stopping I ran straight up the steps to the open front door and on into the hallway. A number of servants were standing around as if waiting for something to happen, though none made any move to greet me or help me off with my coat and hat. They seemed stunned into inaction by some tragic event which had obviously touched them closely.

For a moment I wondered what to do next. I turned to the nearest servant and was about to speak when a door opened at the far end of the hall and an elderly man whom I judged to be the butler entered. Instead of inquiring who I was and what I was doing there, he said abruptly, "You're the detective, are you?"

I was taken aback by this, and was debating how I should reply when a voice behind me said, "No, Jameson, this is Mr. Ross, a friend of mine."

Coming down the stairs towards me was Margaret Trelawney.

She seemed to have aged ten years in the short time that had passed since our last meeting. She arrived at the bottom of the steps and held out her hand.

I rushed forward and took it, ashamed that even as I did so I was unable to stop myself from glancing down to see if there were any signs of bloodstains. To my great relief, there were none. But my feelings of relief did not last long. Her next words made my blood run cold.

"Thank you for coming so quickly, Mr. Ross. Someone has tried to murder my father."

THREE
The Dream Comes to Life

For a moment I was lost for what to say. Her eyes were staring into mine. When I did speak it can only have been a disappointment to her.

"Are you sure it was an attempt at murder? Not some kind of accident?"

Miss Trelawney let her eyes drop to the ground for a few seconds. When she looked up again her face was quite composed.

"It was quite definitely an attempt at murder. What is more, I feel certain that the danger is by no means over. There will be other attempts. Perhaps even before the night is out. Now, please come with me."

Turning, she made her way slowly back upstairs, and I followed.

At the top of the first flight of stairs we walked along a corridor which led to another part of the house. There she began to climb a second staircase.

I was immediately struck by the fact that the corridors of this dark, dusty house were lined with glass cases filled with relics taken from the land of the Pharaohs and the Sphinx, possibly a better and more varied collection than I had seen the previous day at the British Museum. It seemed that only the larger items, such as the great stone sarcophagi and the painted wooden coffins, were missing. However, I soon discovered that I was jumping to the wrong conclusions. At the top of the second flight of stairs was another corridor lined with just such burial cases, at least one of which appeared to have a mummified body still inside it. These large exhibits were set back in alcoves along the corridor, and as the weak light of early morning had not yet penetrated these dark corners I had to look hard to see exactly what was hidden there.

Ahead of me Miss Trelawney had stopped outside a door to allow me to catch up. In a lowered voice she whispered, "If you will just wait here for a moment, I will check with the doctor that it is all right for you to come in."

She opened the door and disappeared inside, taking the light with her.

As I waited for her to reappear I checked back along the corridor. In one small alcove, rather like a cupboard without doors, my eyes had caught a glint of light, possibly a reflection from a small jewel or a piece of broken glass.

A few steps returned me to the place, and I knelt down to look in. It was a deeper recess than I had thought, possibly going back some five feet or more into the wall. At first I could see nothing and presumed that I had been mistaken, but as I began to get to my feet again my eyes glimpsed the greenish glint that I had seen before.

This time it was quite some distance back, so dropping to my knees I reached in as far as I could to investigate.

The next thing I knew there was a piercing screech and an agony of pain in my hand. At the same instant something shot forward out of the alcove and off along the corridor. Immediately the door opened and Margaret ran out of the room. Before I could get to my feet she was down by my side.

"What is it?" she said with alarm. "Are you hurt? What happened?"

"I don't know," I said, clutching my hand to my chest. The pain had lessened now but was still noticeable.

Gently she eased my hand away.

"Here, let me see," she insisted.

As she took her hand from mine, I could see that there was blood on both her hand and mine. At first I was not sure who was bleeding. Then, with a note of relief in her voice she said, "It's all right. It's just a scratch. It looks worse than it is. I'm afraid it was Silvio. You must have frightened him."

"Silvio?" I asked confused.

"My cat." She smiled. "He sometimes hides away in odd corners. I'm sure he didn't mean to hurt you."

"I'm sure he didn't," I said, wrapping my handkerchief around the wound and feeling stupid for making so much fuss over a mere cat scratch.

Miss Trelawney looked at me and smiled for the first time that night. "The doctor said you can come in now. But please, make as little noise as possible."

"Of course." I followed her into the room.

It was certainly not a typical bedroom. There was a bed, yes, with a screen drawn around it. There was also a sofa, and on this lay the body of a man whose upper part was hidden from my view by the doctor who was busy attending to him. Two large wardrobes appeared to be the only other items of furniture usually found in a bedroom.

19

Besides these there was a wall safe, a desk, several easy chairs, a table piled high with books, jars of chemicals and various other items of scientific equipment, and a large traveling trunk. In addition, the room was lined with shelves and cases crammed full of still more relics of ancient Egypt, including the mummified cat Miss Trelawney had told me about in the British Museum. All this my eyes took in the moment I stepped through the door.

But on the far side of the room stood another object that I had not expected to see, yet having found it I could not tear my eyes away. For there—returning from my nightmare world to haunt me—was the mummy's sarcophagus that I had last seen in my dream!

FOUR
The Doctor

I stood frozen to the spot, transfixed by this nightmare vision made real. I felt myself swaying on my feet and reached out to steady myself. My blindly clutching hand struck something, and the next instant the room was filled with the sound of smashing glass as a vase crashed to the floor.

"You idiot!" a voice snapped out. "There is a very sick man here. If you are unable to conduct yourself in a more seemly manner, I shall have to ask you to leave the room."

It was the doctor who had spoken. He had jumped to his feet and was now standing by the side of the couch, glaring angrily in my direction. I felt my face color a bright red. I was deeply embarrassed.

"I'm sorry," I stammered. "My arm caught it. I had no intention of . . ."

The doctor looked at me as though I was a total fool. Then, with a despairing shake of his head, he turned his attention back to his patient.

I looked apologetically at Miss Trelawney, who had remained silent. She lifted her eyebrows and gave a slight shrug of the shoulders.

"It was an accident," she said simply.

I crouched down to pick up the larger pieces of glass, and she knelt beside me to help.

21

"I'm sorry," I whispered. "It really was very clumsy of me. I shall pay for the vase, of course."

"There's no need," she replied, keeping her voice low. "It wasn't very old."

This remark made me feel much better. In this strange house full of ancient, and no doubt priceless, objects the old items were far more valuable than the new.

"I felt slightly dizzy, that's all. I'm not used to being up and around so early in the morning, I'm afraid."

The doctor had moved away from his patient and was searching through his bag. This gave me my first clear view of the figure on the couch, whom I presumed to be Margaret's father.

He was a tall, well-built man, perhaps fifty-five or sixty years of age. His hair was still dark, though graying slightly at the temples. His skin was weatherbeaten, as though he had spent a considerable part of his life outdoors in the open air, but as he lay there now he looked extremely pale.

There was no obvious major injury to the body that I could see. No battering to the head or face. No wounds to the body. The only bandaging was around the man's wrist, which struck me as being a most unusual place for an attacker to inflict an injury.

The doctor returned to the bedside with his wooden stethoscope. Carefully he placed the cupped end against the patient's chest before bending over and applying his right ear to the other end. For a few moments he listened intently, then with a slight nod of satisfaction he straightened up.

"I think we can rest easy for a little while. His

breathing and heartbeat are normal again. He's in no immediate danger."

Miss Trelawney moved immediately to the bedside and took hold of her father's hand. She was obviously greatly relieved. She leaned over and kissed his brow, then studied his face deeply.

"You say his breathing and heartbeat are normal. But what about the rest of him?" she asked.

The doctor was packing his equipment back into his bag and for a few seconds he did not reply.

"Miss Trelawney, you can see that your father is unconscious. I say 'unconscious,' not asleep. He is in some kind of coma. Why? I don't know. There are no injuries to the head."

Here the doctor closed up his bag before continuing. "How long this state will last I cannot say. There are individuals who remain in such a condition for many years, some even until their death. It's possible—not likely, I think, but possible—that this will be the case with your father. I simply do not know at this stage."

The doctor picked up his hat and gloves.

"Now—I think it would be better for the patient if he were able to recover in peace. This place has been more like a railway station than a sickroom over the past half-hour," he said, looking at me. "Perhaps it would be better if we conducted our discussions elsewhere."

"Of course," Miss Trelawney agreed, opening the door. "I shall ask the housekeeper to sit by the bed in case there is any change in my father's condition."

As we came to the top of the stairs, a middle-aged woman was hurrying up the last few steps. She was obviously somewhat upset.

"Sorry to bother you, miss," she said, "but there's someone to see you downstairs."

"Who is it, Mrs. Grant?"

"He says he's a detective, miss. And he's arrested Jackson the gate porter."

FIVE
The Mysterious Attack

The detective was waiting for us in the drawing room. He immediately introduced himself to Miss Trelawney.

"Sergeant Daw, miss," he said. "Sergeant Daw of Scotland Yard."

"I am pleased to meet you, sergeant," she replied. "Thank you for coming so quickly. I am Margaret Trelawney. It is my father who has suffered this mysterious attack. My housekeeper tells me you have arrested one of my servants."

"Not arrested, Miss Trelawney," Sergeant Daw said with a slight smile. "Just taken him away for questioning. You see, he was convicted about two years ago, for theft. Spent some time in Brixton Prison as a result."

This information hit me like a bombshell.

"Of course," I exclaimed. "That's where I've seen him. In court."

"That's right, sir," the detective nodded. "I believe you were there the day he was sent down."

In the excitement of Sergeant Daw's arrival, Miss Trelawney had obviously quite forgotten that the doctor and I were there.

"I must apologize. I quite forgot to introduce you," she said. "Sergeant Daw, this is Dr. Winchester. And this is . . ."

"That's all right, miss," the detective interrupted, "I already know Mr. Ross. We worked together on a case of poisoning in Hoxton." Then, seeing the doctor's surprise, he added, "Not to worry, doctor. Mr. Ross is a gentleman of the court—a lawyer. He cross-examined me in a case of attempted murder—on the effect of arsenic. Questioned me very thoroughly, as well, if you don't mind me saying so."

"A very interesting case if I remember rightly, sergeant," I said. "I hope there's no hard feeling over the questioning."

"None at all." The sergeant smiled. "Just doing your job. And besides, unless I'm very much mistaken, your client was found guilty."

Dr. Winchester looked at me and grinned.

"Can't win them all," he said.

I ignored this remark. "So you think the man at the gate may have been responsible for this attack on Miss Trelawney's father, sergeant?"

Sergeant Daw shook his head.

"I'm not saying that, Mr. Ross. Not now. All I'm saying is that a known criminal is guarding the gate of a house where a crime has taken place. Now, if he's guilty, he's not going to wait around for me to make my investigations, is he? No, by the time I've done that, he's going to have disappeared."

"If he'd done what you imply, don't you think he would already have disappeared?" Margaret's voice rang out across the room.

"Possibly so, miss. But if he's innocent he's got nothing to hide. At the present time all I know is what Constable Hooper reported on the journey over here. So perhaps, Miss Trelawney, you'll tell me exactly what's happened."

26

Miss Trelawney sat down.

"Of course, sergeant. It will take some time for me to tell my story, so please, gentlemen, be seated."

We took our places around the side of the room, and Miss Trelawney began her tale.

"I'm not sure what woke me, just that I was jolted out of my sleep. I sat up with a start and felt certain that something was wrong. Then I heard a noise. At first I thought it was someone in my room, but as I listened I realized that it was in fact coming from the room next door—my father's room. Immediately I felt relieved. You see, my father often works unusual hours. Very late at night. Sometimes early in the morning. At any rate I often hear him moving around."

"And what does he do at these hours?"

Miss Trelawney looked at him for a few seconds, then replied, "I'm afraid I have no idea, sergeant."

"No idea?"

"None. I have only recently come to live here with him. My mother died when I was born, and I was brought up by my aunt. My father came to visit me whenever he could, of course, but he has spent much of his time abroad. As a result we are strangers in many ways. I certainly know nothing of his work apart from what anyone could discover by looking around the house. He is passionately interested in the civilization of ancient Egypt, and I believe that many people consider him to be a great authority on the subject."

Miss Trelawney was obviously upset at having to admit she knew so little about her father. I tried gently to return her to the matter in hand.

"You say you were not worried when you first realized that the noise came from the next room?"

"No, not at first."

27

"So when did you become worried?"

"As I listened—there in the dark—I realized that the noise was not the normal sounds that someone moving around would make."

"In what way, miss?" the detective asked.

"It was a dragging noise."

"As though someone was moving furniture?"

"No." She shook her head. "More as though a body was being pulled around."

"A body!" I echoed. "What did you do?"

"I got out of bed and quietly made my way over to the door that divides my room from my father's. I stood there listening. The noise was more distinct, and there was also the terrible sound of strained breathing. As though some horrible, legless monster was dragging itself about the room. I was terrified. I turned the handle and pushed open the door. There was no light on in the room. It was quite dark."

"The breathing," the detective asked, "could you still hear it?"

"More clearly than ever, as if someone or something was desperately fighting for every breath."

Miss Trelawney shivered as she relived the moment.

"And all the time it was coming nearer. Pulling itself across the floor toward me. I tried to scream, but I couldn't. I reached out behind me for something to defend myself with, but there was nothing there. Then my hand touched the switch, and I turned on the light. What I saw terrified me."

At this point Miss Trelawney was overcome with the horror of the memory and had to pause for a moment. On the table was a pitcher of water and some glasses, so I poured out a glass and handed it to her. She looked up at me and nodded her thanks. I sat down again. The room was filled with tension as we waited for her to continue. She took a single sip and carried on.

"The first thing I saw was the bed. It was empty. No sign of my father. Just a mass of crumpled sheets. And in the middle of it an enormous dark red stain— spreading down over the edge—glistening in the light. There was no doubt about it—it was blood. I tracked it from the bed across the room to the safe, and that's where I found my father, lying in more blood.

"He was on his right side with his other arm twisted underneath him, as though his body had been hurled down there in a heap and left for dead. The only major injury seemed to be to his wrist, where the flesh was ripped and torn and blood was pumping out in angry spurts. That sight finally spurred me to action. I ran to the top of the stairs and yelled for help as loudly as I could. I screamed. I shouted. And at last the servants came. The rest you know. Mrs. Grant attended to my father while I made arrangements to get help from outside."

Sergeant Daw stood up.

"Now, Miss Trelawney, you say your father works strange hours," he said. "How long has this been going on?"

"When did it start, you mean? It was just after the visitor."

"What visitor?"

"I can't give you his name, I'm afraid, nor a description. I did not actually meet the gentleman. But I heard him."

"Heard him? Perhaps you could explain."

"It was in the early hours of the morning—just three months ago yesterday. I was in bed when I was awakened by the bell at the outside gate. A few minutes

29

later there was a knocking at the door, and I heard my father leave his room and walk along the corridor to the stairs. A short while later he returned, but this time there was a second set of footsteps as well."

"And they went into your father's room?" Sergeant Daw asked, obviously intrigued by this new information.

"Yes. I could hear them speaking."

"Arguing?"

"No. Talking loudly—excitedly—but not arguing. Eventually I drifted back to sleep with the sound of their voices still in my ears. When I awoke the next morning the conversation was still going on, though more sporadically than before. They stayed in there the whole of the next day. I knocked on the door toward evening to ask my father if there was anything wrong, but he said I should leave them alone—he would send for me if he wanted anything."

"He opened the door to say this?" I inquired.

"Just a few inches."

"Did you see the other man?"

Miss Trelawney only hesitated for a moment, but Sergeant Daw was quick to spot it.

"You must tell us anything you saw, miss. No matter what. The slightest detail could be a vital clue."

"I did not see the man," she answered slowly. "But I did see his coat. It was thrown over a chair. I glimpsed it through the crack in the door when my father opened it. It was a traveler's coat."

"A traveler's coat?" I asked, feeling quite stupid at not understanding what she meant by this.

"Yes, Mr. Ross," she answered kindly. "The kind of coat that a man would wear when traveling abroad in very warm climates. I know—my father has one himself which he wears on his journeys to Egypt."

"Then are you sure it wasn't his? Your father's?" I asked.

She shook her head, quite certain of herself.

Sergeant Daw had been writing in his notebook. Now he looked up.

"Did you not ask your father about this stranger, Miss Trelawney?"

"I did."

"And his reply?"

"He said simply that a colleague had visited him whom he had not seen for some time, and they had had much to discuss."

"And that was the end of it? You did not press him further?"

"My father, sergeant, was . . . is . . . not a man who is easily pressed. When he indicates that a conversation is at an end, it is at an end."

"I see. And this stranger, has he returned to the house at any time since, so far as you know?"

"No." Miss Trelawney was quite definite in her reply. "Since that time my father has seen no one other than members of this household. He has been too busy working."

At this point, Sergeant Daw appeared to decide that this line of questioning had gone far enough. Putting his notebook in his pocket, he walked across the room to the door and opened it.

"I should now like to examine the scene of the crime, Miss Trelawney," he said.

SIX

The Scene of the Crime

As we entered the room, Mrs. Grant rose from her seat at the foot of the sofa and quietly went out. Mr. Trelawney lay as we had left him some half an hour earlier, still breathing deeply and regularly, flat on his back, his right arm at his side. His left, heavily bandaged, rested across his chest.

Sergeant Daw took a long, hard look at him, then turned back to Miss Trelawney. "This dragging sound, miss—are you sure it came from your father's room?"

"Where else could it come from?"

"From the corridor outside, perhaps?"

She shook her head. "I am as certain as I can be sergeant. Whatever that noise was, it came from this room."

"When did the sound stop?"

She paused, deep in thought. "When I put the light on."

He added something to his notebook, then put his pencil away.

"Thank you, miss," he said. "Now I'll get on with my examination of the room, if you have no objection."

His inspection began with the bed. Using a magnifying glass he looked carefully at the folds of the sheets, then at the heavily stained area in the middle. This he touched with his fingers as if to make sure it really was blood.

Moving around to the other side of the bed he followed the trail of red across the floor to where the body had been discovered just in front of the great safe. He examined the double doors of the safe, around the lock and along the top and bottom, and especially where they met in the center. He shook his head as though puzzled by what he had found before moving to the far side of the room to check each window in turn.

At last he addressed Dr. Winchester. "I should be grateful, doctor, if you could now give me a full report on the patient. Leave out no detail, please. However small."

"Of course." The doctor cleared his throat and began. "Mr. Trelawney has only one wound to his body. Here, at the left wrist. That is to say, there are actually two separate wounds close together—so close that at first I was unable to see that they were distinct. Near the base of the thumb there are a series of scratch marks which run in a straight line across the wrist— fine but deep—obviously caused by a very sharp instrument. A little higher up the arm there is a deep, jagged wound where the skin is bruised and torn rather than sliced—gouged as if by a blunt instrument. It was this which damaged the veins and led to the loss of blood."

"Is that why the patient is still unconscious, doctor?" the detective asked.

"No, I think not. In fact, I have no real idea why Mr. Trelawney is in this state. There is no wound or bruising to the head, so he cannot be concussed."

"Anything else?"

"Only this!" Dr. Winchester leaned over and pulled back the ripped left sleeve of Mr. Trelawney's nightshift. There, just above the bandaging, was a round silver bangle.

"This bangle was cutting into the skin quite deeply —but it is no ordinary bangle. It looks like silver but is in reality the strongest triple-forged steel with a silver coating. There are marks on it where I believe someone has tried to file through it—unsuccessfully, of course."

"But why would anyone want to do that?" I burst out. "Surely it's of no great value."

"None," said the doctor. "Unless you want this key that is on it."

"Key!" Sergeant Daw exclaimed.

"A key to what?" I shouted excitedly.

"To the safe, of course," Dr. Winchester replied. "I'd say that whoever attacked Mr. Trelawney was after the key to his safe. When they couldn't get the key from the bangle they attempted to cut through the wrist. This also failed, so they dragged the poor man from the bed and tried to reach the safe's lock with the key still on his wrist."

"But Miss Trelawney disturbed them before they could manage it," I said.

"We don't know that, Mr. Ross," the sergeant said. "Not as yet. For all we know they could have been successful in opening the safe and locked it again after them."

Here, Miss Trelawney, who had been badly shaken

by this news, spoke. "How could this have happened when I saw no one in the room?"

"Begging your pardon, miss, but with professional criminals you rarely—if ever—see anyone. Either he made his escape from the room before you even opened the door, or when you entered the room he hid himself until you left it again to call for the servants."

Here the detective turned to the doctor. "Is that all you have to report then, Dr. Winchester?"

"I would have thought that was enough, sergeant," the doctor smiled.

"Yes, indeed," Sergeant Daw said. "Miss Trelawney, do you have any objection to my examining the contents of your father's desk?"

Miss Trelawney shook her head but said nothing. She was clearly beginning to feel the strain of the night's happenings.

Sergeant Daw at once began a systematic search of the cluttered desk. First, he went through all the items that filled every inch of space on top, then, finding nothing of significance there, he went carefully through each of the desk drawers.

He had reached the final drawer without finding anything to excite his interest when suddenly he stopped dead in his tracks. For a few seconds he looked down into the drawer, then, reaching inside, he pulled out an envelope.

"This is addressed to you, Miss Trelawney," he said. "I think you had better read it."

SEVEN
The Letter

My dear daughter,

As you are now reading this letter I can only assume that some terrible event has happened to me. I must tell you that this is not unexpected. I have known for several months that strange things were likely to occur without being certain of what they would prove to be.

As I must be unable to help myself, it is now up to you to look after my safety. My life, if I am still alive, depends on you.

I rely on you to carry out the instructions which are part of this letter. I cannot emphasize too strongly that they must be followed to the last detail. Let no one persuade you to do otherwise or my life will be at risk.

Obey the following commands without question.

First: if I am not in my bedroom when my body is discovered, see that I am moved there as quickly as possible. Even if I am dead, take my corpse to that room and place it on the bed.

Do not move the bed from the position it is already in (if you are in any doubt, look on the floor; you will find marks where the four legs are to stand).

When this has been done, make sure that I am

never left alone until either I regain consciousness, or I am buried in my grave. During the day make sure that at least one person is always with me. From nightfall to sunrise—the danger hours—this number should be increased to two, one man and one woman. Always—without fail—one of each sex.

Second: it is essential that nothing in my room is moved or disturbed in any way.

Every object has its specific place. If anything has already been moved when I am discovered, replace it in its position as soon as possible. To help with this task I am including a plan of the room which shows the exact place for every item other than my papers, which are of no importance. Again, do not be persuaded otherwise—not if you value my life.

My third instruction is this. Immediately contact a friend whom you feel you can trust. Ask him to spend as much time in the house with you as possible. He may help you in your task of looking over me.

If either of you has to leave the house for any reason, be back before nightfall. Once it is dark, do not leave the house. Your own safety may depend upon this.

Finally my lawyers, Marvin and Jewkes of 27B Lincoln's Inn Fields, have full instructions in case of my death. Mr. Marvin has personally agreed to carry out my wishes. He is also aware that strange or unusual events may befall me. You might find it useful to seek his advice.

I appreciate that this is very difficult for you to understand. I am sorry that I cannot be more clear in my explanation. Try not to be afraid for my safety.

My life may well be in danger, but I am quite certain that my actions are essential if my life's work is not to be wasted.

I pray that one day we shall meet again.

Until then, trust in me.

Your loving father,
Abel Trelawney.

As Miss Trelawney finished reading, she folded the letter and passed it over to Sergeant Daw, who immediately read the contents through for himself before handing it back to her.

Eventually it was Dr. Winchester who broke the silence.

"I knew that there was something strange going on here. I felt it as soon as I arrived in the house. This letter proves it."

Sergeant Daw's reaction was nothing if not unexpected.

"No, doctor," he said. "The letter proves nothing except that Mr. Trelawney feared for his safety. That is hardly unusual, is it? Not in a house so full of treasures and priceless relics. To keep so much of value in a house like this is asking for trouble. Obviously Mr. Trelawney realized that the chances of being robbed at some time and perhaps injured in the process were very high. Unfortunately, it has now happened."

Dr. Winchester looked as though he could hardly believe his ears. He stared open-mouthed at Sergeant Daw, not knowing what to say. I could well understand his reaction. I, too, was astounded.

"Are you saying, sergeant, that you think this has all been the result of a burglary?"

Sergeant Daw was guarded in his answer. "I think that possible, Mr. Ross. Don't you?"

I hardly knew how to reply. "Possible," I said. "Yes. Almost anything is possible. But it hardly seems likely."

"Likely!" the doctor exploded. "The very idea is preposterous. A body is found in a room where there is no sign of forced entry. Then a letter is found in which the victim not only warns that this is likely to happen but also gives the most mysterious set of instructio⟩ ͂ one is ever likely to find—and the conclusion that you reach is what? Burglary!"

I think I have never seen anyone look as uncomfortable as the police sergeant at that moment and, even though I had to agree with everything Dr. Winchester had said, I felt I must defend him.

"Of course, sergeant, in one way you are right," I said. "We must keep an open mind about the matter— investigate all possibilities."

"Nonsense," the doctor snapped.

"Nevertheless," I continued, "our task now is to consider what we are going to do in the light of the letter."

Here Miss Trelawney stood up, clutching the paper firmly in her hand.

"There is no doubt about what we are going to do, Mr. Ross," she said. "We are going to follow the instructions. You may be willing to put my father's life at risk, but I most certainly am not."

Dr. Winchester beamed at this statement.

"Bravo, Miss Trelawney," he said. "At least there is someone here who is not afraid to look into the unknown. As far as I am concerned, I shall be willing to help you in every way I can."

"Oh, I don't doubt that we should follow the instructions in the letter," I stammered, feeling myself going red around the collar. "All I meant was that we must try and keep an open mind about what has happened until we have more evidence."

"Typical lawyer," the doctor sneered. "Fine in a courtroom, but next to useless in real life."

"Now look here, Dr. Winchester," I began, but before I could finish Miss Trelawney had cut in.

"You are both right. We must take note of what my father says in his letter, yet at the same time we must be willing to consider every possibility. In which case, Mr. Ross, I wonder if you would grant me one more favor."

"Of course," I said. "What is it?"

When I heard the words that followed my heart leapt for joy.

"I would like you to be the friend my father advises me to take—to stay here with me until this business is completed. Can I count on you for that—Malcolm?"

EIGHT
The Gunshots

From that moment on we began to put Mr. Trelawney's instructions into effect. Servants were called to remove the bloodstained sheets and mattress and to replace them with clean ones. Once this was done, Dr. Winchester, Sergeant Daw, Margaret, and myself lifted the inert body of Mr. Trelawney from the couch where it had been lying on to the newly made bed.

Margaret and I then began the task of examining the plan of the room and making sure that everything marked on it was still in its correct place. We knew this had to be done very carefully, and it took us the best part of the morning to complete.

While we did this Dr. Winchester went off to attend to his practice and find a nurse who could come in and help to look after his patient. Sergeant Daw returned to the police station to question Jackson, the gate porter.

When Margaret and I had finished checking the contents of the room—we found nothing missing and nothing out of place—we called for Mrs. Grant to take over from us and made our way downstairs. Over lunch we discussed the things that still needed to be done.

Firstly, a rotation had to be worked out to ensure that there was always someone sitting with Margaret's father. It was relatively easy to sort out the daylight hours, when only one person at a time was needed. But at night, when there had to be two people present at all times, a man and a woman, it was much more difficult. Even so, after deciding that each watch should last three hours, we were able to work out a pattern which we thought could be kept going for several weeks if need be.

At this point it seemed that there was nothing more I could do for the moment, and so I, too, returned to my room to collect enough clothes and belongings to last me several days.

I also called in at my office to warn the clerks that I would not be available until further notice, and to leave the address where I might be contacted. Needless to say, there was no outstanding work waiting for me, and they were not at all perturbed by my likely absence. So it was with a sense of relief that I was useful to one person at least that I returned to the Trelawneys' house.

When I arrived, Margaret was sitting with her father. I went into the library to pass the time until she finished her watch.

The walls were lined with books about ancient Egypt. I took a few down from the shelves and leafed through them. In several there were passages marked in pencil and comments written in the margins. I tried to make some sense of them, but found that I knew too little about Egyptian life and civilization to understand.

As I was so engaged the door opened and Sergeant Daw entered. He was clearly agitated about something, but at first he made no mention of what was worrying him. Instead he filled in the time by talking of past cases. Then, suddenly, he changed the subject.

"What do you think of this business, Mr. Ross?"

"I think there must be some sensible explanation, but at the moment I must admit I don't see what it is," I replied.

"Of course," Sergeant Daw continued, "it would all be a good deal clearer if only I could get this man Jackson to talk."

Suddenly I realized what was really troubling the detective. He had spent the greater part of the afternoon questioning his chief—and as yet only—suspect, and had clearly made little progress.

"He has nothing to say?" I asked.

"Oh, he's got plenty to say all right. Says he knows nothing about it—he had nothing to do with it, and has witnesses to prove as much."

"And has he?"

"One of the footmen. Sat up in the gatehouse with him, keeping him company. No doubt the two of them are in it together."

"In that case, sergeant, shouldn't you have taken the footman in as well? What if he tries to get away?"

"That's just what I'm hoping for, sir. That'd be the proof I need. I've got a man watching the house. There'll be no escape—that's one thing I'm certain of."

At that moment there was a noise in the corridor outside, and the library door was flung open. It was Dr. Winchester, accompanied by a woman dressed in a black cloak and bonnet.

"This is Nurse Kennedy," he announced. "Where is Miss Trelawney?"

"She's with her father," I said. "I'll go and get her."

I left the room and ran up the two flights of stairs and along the corridor. As quietly as I could, I opened the door and entered.

Margaret was sitting on a chair at the foot of the bed. She was reading and had not heard me come in. I tiptoed across to where she sat and gently touched her shoulder. She gasped with shock and twisted her head around to see who or what had suddenly appeared at her side.

As she did so she let go of the book and it clattered to the floor. Both of us looked immediately at the patient, but he lay just as he had done twelve hours earlier, registering nothing of the outside world.

Margaret was breathing heavily, and her eyes had a strange look in them, as though my unexpected entrance had suddenly brought her out of a trance.

"I'm sorry," I said. "I didn't mean to startle you. Are you all right?"

She was still trying to catch her breath, and her eyes were puzzled, unsure of what was going on.

"Yes, I think so. You just took me by surprise. I was reading, and . . ."

Her voice died away, and she bent down to pick up the book she had dropped. When she looked at me again she had regained her control.

"What is it? Is something wrong?"

"No," I answered. "There's nothing wrong. It's simply that Dr. Winchester has returned. He's brought the nurse with him and would like to see you downstairs. I'll take over until the end of your shift."

She glanced at the clock.

"Thank you," she said, standing up and touching my arm. "It's only another half-hour."

And with that she left the room.

I sat down in the chair she had just vacated. Mr. Trelawney lay on the bed, his bandaged wrist on top of the bedclothes. His breathing continued slowly and regularly, his face still expressionless, his body quite immobile.

For a little while I stared around the room at the many objects that filled every nook and cranny, every shelf, every flat surface. The majority of these were small: exquisitely carved stones, tiny statues and models —all, no doubt, taken from the tomb of some long dead prince or pharaoh.

But there were also larger items: the stone sarcophagus I had first seen in my dream, two painted wooden coffins, and a number of mummified bodies. Despite their glass cases, they still gave off the heavy chemical smells I had come to associate with them.

I found myself wondering about the events of the night. Going over every detail again and again— looking for an explanation that fitted in with my ideas of what was possible in the world. I was becoming less and less conscious of the room and the body lying on the bed in front of me.

A sudden noise from the street outside jerked me out of these musings. Looking at the clock I saw it was some fifteen minutes past the hour when I was due to be relieved. Time had passed without my noticing it. Certainly I was tired from my lack of sleep, but was there something about that room—or something *in* the room—which had had the effect of making me drift into a semi-conscious state? Hadn't Margaret also seemed less than attentive when I had entered a little while earlier?

But what could be causing this reaction? And if I felt like this after sitting for half an hour or so in daylight, how much worse would it be during the long hours of darkness?

My thoughts were suddenly interrupted by the

arrival of Sergeant Daw and Mrs. Grant. They were to do the first of the nighttime watches; then Nurse Kennedy and myself, and finally Dr. Winchester and Margaret.

I stood up and went downstairs to say goodnight to Margaret, but to my disappointment she had already gone to bed. Dr. Winchester had also departed. He had been called out to see another patient, but had left a message to say that he was unlikely to be more than an hour. So, after first arranging for one of the servants to call me thirty minutes before I was due to begin my watch, I went to my room and lay down.

Within minutes I was asleep, and the next thing I knew I was being roughly shaken by the shoulder.

"Mr. Ross! Mr. Ross! Wake up! It's midnight, sir."

I tried desperately to bring myself to my senses but sleep had a strong hold on my body and was reluctant to let go. Still half-asleep, I tried to swing my legs off the bed. I think the servant must have helped me, because without knowing how I got there I found I was on my feet and being walked around the room. Soon I was able to disentangle myself from the servant's grasp and stand properly on my own.

"I thought for a moment that you was gone as well, Mr. Ross." The servant was grinning with relief.

"No, no, I'm quite all right. Really," I said. "Thank you for waking me. I can manage now."

The servant went out of the room, leaving me alone. I opened the window and took in several gulps of fresh air. I had to be as alert as possible before beginning my vigil. The cool sharp breeze did its job, and when I closed the window again my mind was working at top speed.

I decided that I had to find some way of lessening the

effects of the fumes in that room. I opened a drawer and looked through the few items of clothing that I had brought with me. I selected a black silk scarf and a large white cotton handkerchief, put them in my pocket and went off to relieve Sergeant Daw.

When I arrived I found that Nurse Kennedy had already taken over from Mrs. Grant. She was sitting at the foot of the bed, while the detective was seated against the wall where he was in a position to see everything in the room. He did not move.

I touched him on the shoulder. He did not exactly jump, but I felt sure that he had to summon every ounce of self-control not to react. It was as though he had not seen me approach, yet I had walked straight across his line of vision.

When he looked up at me, there was a look of guilt in his eyes.

"I wasn't asleep," he whispered.

"I never dreamed you were," I replied, trying to keep my voice as quiet as I could. "I'm sorry if I'm late."

The sergeant shook his head.

"You're not," he said. "She"—nodding toward the nurse—"was early."

With that he stood up and left the room. I sat down and checked my watch. It was two minutes to one.

Slowly I looked around the room. It was definitely no place for anyone with a lively imagination. It was all too easy to believe in the unbelievable, sitting there in the semi-darkness, surrounded by the remains of a civilization born several thousand years ago in a far distant and magical land.

The smell in the room was quite overpowering, and I found myself wondering if it was somehow connected with Mr. Trelawney's illness. After all, if the pungent aroma of the chemicals had affected me when I had been in the room for less than half an hour, how much more might it have affected someone who seemed to spend the greater part of his life breathing that atmosphere?

With this in mind, I removed the silk scarf and the cotton handkerchief from my jacket pocket. I folded the scarf in half lengthways and the handkerchief into a square pad measuring roughly six inches by six. This gave four thicknesses of material. Then I pressed the handkerchief against my face so that both my nose and mouth were covered, securing it in position with the scarf. In this way, the air that I was breathing was being filtered through six layers of material.

This done, my thoughts once again began to wander, only to be brought abruptly back to the present by a sudden noise. There was a rustling sound over to my left, and my nerves began to jangle.

One of the curtains seemed to be moving.

Startled, I sat bolt upright on my seat and looked quickly around for something to defend myself with should the necessity arise. But I could see nothing that was likely to be of any use.

Again the movement of the curtain.

I felt sure there was someone over in that part of the room.

Could somebody have gotten in through the window without my realizing it?

Surely that was not possible. I could not have failed to hear the window open. But what if he had already been in the room when I began my duty? Just waiting for me to come in so that he could make his attack on me when I was not expecting it?

Then a still more unpleasant thought struck me. What if the sound was not coming from the window, as I thought, but from the great stone sarcophagus? Somehow my dream must have foretold what was going to happen to me.

Perhaps the sound was coming from inside it. Perhaps, just as in my nightmare, the mummy enclosed within that ancient stone casket was even now coming to life. Any moment now the lid would begin to rise and the fingers of that hand would come creeping over the edge.

My mind was beginning to slip away from the present, toward a kind of hazy dream world. I was still in the room—that much I knew—but it seemed far more like a vision than reality.

Nurse Kennedy was sitting in front of me, motionless. Still and silent as the grave. In fact the whole room was unnaturally quiet. Then, suddenly, a sound began to cut through the silence. It was the tortured rasping breath of a man fighting for his life.

And it was coming from the bed.

I tried to stand so that I could raise the alarm, but my legs would not obey the orders that my brain was sending to them.

My senses were now awhirl. Again I thought I heard the rustling sound, and also the distant mewing of a cat. Then a clink of metal—and finally an explosion of sound and a blaze of light which seemed to fill the room. This jerked me back to reality and I leaped to my feet just in time to see another explosion of light and the unmistakable crack of a pistol.

Someone in that room was firing a gun.

NINE
The Ghostly Figure

Smoke from the pistol shots filled the room, and there was a confusion of voices and figures everywhere. I made a move to step forward, but somehow my legs were still not responding as they should, and I ended up in a half-kneeling position on the floor.

There the smoke was less dense and I was able to see more clearly what was going on.

The sight that met my eyes was quite terrifying. Mr. Trelawney lay stretched out across the floor, his injured arm pointing toward the wall safe. The bandages that had been protecting his wound had been ripped off and were lying scattered around him, tattered and blood-stained. His wrist was spurting blood, both from the old wound, which had reopened, and from a new cut higher up the arm.

By the side of his mangled limb, its point embedded in the floor, was the weapon that had inflicted this new outrage. It was a double-edged, leaf-shaped "kukri" knife of the type used by Indian soldiers in the Far East. I had noticed it earlier in the day, mounted on the wall. But it had been taken down from its place, and an attempt had been made to cut through the arm completely, so that the bangle that held the key to the safe could be removed.

Fortunately, this attempt had not been successful, as the main force of the blow had been taken by the floor. Even so, the flesh was cut through to the bone. At least one artery had been severed; blood was pumping out in regular spurts so that quite a pool of blood had already formed around the body.

Margaret was kneeling by her father's side, her white nightdress rapidly becoming soaked in blood as she leaned over him, trying to apply pressure to the upper arm to slow the blood loss from the wounds.

Above her was the figure of Sergeant Daw. In his hand was a police-issue revolver, which he was reloading. His eyes were red and heavy. He was clearly dazed by whatever had taken place and was acting in a totally mechanical fashion, barely aware of what was going on around him.

Making a supreme effort, I managed to stagger to my feet and take a few stumbling steps toward Margaret and her father. Margaret must have caught my movement out of the corner of her eye because she suddenly looked up. As she did so, the look on her face changed to one of total panic. She shouted something to Sergeant Daw, then threw herself headlong across her father's body as if to protect him. The detective immediately raised his revolver and pointed it at me.

I hurled myself to one side. There was another explosion of sound and flash of light. Behind me was the crash of smashing glass.

I rolled over on the floor and looked up. Sergeant Daw had twisted around and was once again aiming the gun in my direction. I was totally confused. I could think of no reason at all why he would want to kill me.

Then I realized what it was all about. The scarf and

handkerchief, which were still wrapped around my face, not only hid my true identity but also gave me the appearance of an intruder. Margaret and Sergeant Daw clearly thought that I was the one who had broken into the house and attacked Mr. Trelawney.

In a moment I had wrenched the scarf from my face and shouted, "Don't shoot! It's me—Ross!"

Dumbfounded, Sergeant Daw lowered the gun and stared at me in disbelief. An instant later another figure hurtled through the door toward the body of Mr. Trelawney. This time, however, the detective had the presence of mind to call out before firing.

"Stay where you are, or I'll shoot."

The figure stopped dead in its tracks before answering. "Get a grip on yourself, man. There's been quite enough shooting in here already, to my mind. Now step back. I've got a patient's life to save."

It was Dr. Winchester.

Angrily, he pulled Margaret to her feet. Her nightdress was now heavily stained with her father's blood, which dripped from the hem of the garment down onto her bare toes. Looking across at me, she recognized me at last and her face filled with relief.

Stepping around the body, I took her in my arms to comfort her. She began to cry, burying her bloodsmeared face against my chest.

Dr. Winchester was working feverishly on his patient, who was still losing blood at a frightening rate. As he labored to apply a tourniquet to stop the flow, he looked up at Sergeant Daw.

"What happened—I thought someone was to be with him all the time."

"I was here," I said.

"I might have known," the doctor sneered. "You simply sat and watched, I suppose."

"No, of course not," I snapped back.

"So what is your explanation, Mr. Ross?"

I felt like a complete fool.

"I'm afraid I don't know," I said. "I'm as much in the dark about this as you are."

The doctor shook his head scornfully. "I find that all too easy to believe. Now will someone please get me some clean water to wash these wounds?"

Margaret pushed herself away from me.

"I'll do it," she said.

"No," Dr. Winchester ordered. "Nurse Kennedy, you get it, please."

In the confusion we had forgotten the presence of the nurse, but now that our attention was drawn to her we all turned around. She was still sitting, completely motionless, on the chair at the foot of the bed, apparently quite unaware of the events happening around her.

"Nurse Kennedy," the doctor repeated.

Still there was no response.

Sergeant Daw stepped around to look at her face. He put his hand to her forehead before speaking.

"I think she's dead."

Dr. Winchester's hand went to the nurse's pulse. Then he took out a small pocket mirror and reflected the light from one of the lamps into her eyes.

"She's not dead," he said in a relieved tone, "but in some kind of trance. There's nothing I can do for her at present. Now please—get me water."

The doctor's request was granted almost immediately. At that moment Mrs. Grant entered with a steaming bowl of water and number of clean towels, which she put down by his side.

"Thank you, Mrs. Grant," he said. "At least someone around here is capable of carrying out her duties properly." He looked around at the rest of us. "Now if you don't mind I would like to be left alone to see to my patients. I'm sure I will get all the help I need from Mrs. Grant here. However, if I do require the assistance of anyone else, I will send for him."

And with that he turned his back on us.

Slowly, and with a terrible feeling of depression, we left the room and made our way downstairs to the study. For some minutes we sat there without speaking, stunned by what had occurred.

It was Margaret who eventually broke the silence.

"I don't see how it can have happened," she said, her eyes fixed firmly on me.

I looked to Sergeant Daw for help but he, too, was staring in my direction.

"I'm sorry," I said. "I know it must look as though I was neglecting my duty, but I really have no idea how all this came about."

"Were you attacked, sir? Knocked out?" Sergeant Daw asked.

"I wish I could say I was. But no, nothing of the kind."

"Then what did you see?"

"Again—nothing. The first thing I was aware of was the gunshots—and seeing the body on the floor."

"You mean you were asleep!" Margaret asked incredulously. "You were asleep when you were supposed to be watching over my father?"

"No," I protested. "Really, I wasn't asleep. I swear it. And yet, somehow, my thoughts were not in the room. It was as though my mind had been drawn away so that I should not know what was going on."

"That's rather difficult to believe, sir, if you'll excuse my saying so," said Sergeant Daw. "Are you sure you weren't asleep and dreaming?"

"I was drowsy, sergeant, but not asleep. I'm sure you understand what I mean. Did you not have a similar experience earlier? When I came in to take over, you certainly didn't seem to be in full control of your faculties."

Sergeant Daw looked very awkward at this, but before he could say anything Margaret spoke.

"You need not be ashamed to admit it, sergeant. I think we have all felt a drowsiness after sitting in that room for any length of time."

The policeman hesitated for a moment, then nodded agreement.

"Yes, miss. That's true. I've no idea why it happens, but it does, no matter how hard you try to resist it, so I suppose there's no point in being too hard on Mr. Ross here."

"Very kind of you, I'm sure," I said.

"All the same," the detective continued, "tonight has been a very close shave. It could have ended in disaster had Dr. Winchester not been at hand to deal with the crisis so quickly."

"Quite so," said Margaret. "All the more reason for us to make an attempt to discover exactly what happened. Are you sure you can tell us nothing, Malcolm?"

In a few sentences I outlined the events as I recalled them. It was not difficult or time-consuming—I knew precious little.

"So let me get this straight, sir," Sergeant Daw

recapped. "The only things you remember now are a rustling sound which seemed to be inside the room and the mewing of a cat."

"I'm not certain about the cat," I had to admit. "But I think that's so, yes."

The detective shook his head. "It's not much to go on, I'm afraid," he said wearily.

"What about you? Were you the first on the scene? Or was it you, Margaret?"

"I think it was the sergeant," Margaret said uneasily.

Sergeant Daw looked surprised. "No, miss," he said. "It was you that was there first. Perhaps we could hear your story."

Margaret appeared troubled, as though she was not entirely certain of her facts.

"I think I am too upset to remember very accurately," she said. "But as I recall it, I awoke quite suddenly with the same horrible feeling that my father was in great danger. I jumped out of bed and ran immediately to his room. When I opened the door I realized that it was almost pitch dark. The lights had been put out for some reason."

"Not by me," I interrupted.

"I've no way of knowing," Margaret said. "All I can say is that the lights were out. But enough light spilled in from the corridor to show that the bed was empty and the bedclothes had been thrown untidily to one side. I looked down at the floor and there he lay, just like last time. I think I may have screamed, I'm not sure. The next thing I knew, you were there, sergeant."

"Yes, well, miss, I don't think there's very much I can add." The sergeant was still fiddling nervously with the pistol. "I went to be after my spell on guard and put the gun under my pillow. Some time later I thought I heard a scream. I immediately reached for the gun and set off for Mr. Trelawney's room. On the way I heard a second scream. The door was already open, and I went right in. Miss Trelawney was kneeling on the floor next to her father. It was too dark for me to see his injuries, so I moved toward the light switch, but before I could get to it I thought I saw something move between me and the window. I was still half asleep, dazed, not quite certain what was going on. So I aimed and fired."

"It was you that fired?"

"Yes, sir."

"Both times?"

"Twice, yes."

"Three times, I think," Margaret said.

"Ah, yes." The sergeant looked extremely uncomfortable. "I'm sorry about that, sir."

"Sorry you missed, you mean?" I grinned.

"I didn't realize it was you. Not with that scarf wrapped around your face like that."

"No," I said. "There was no reason why you should, of course. It was an attempt to prevent the fumes from affecting me. Not very successful, I'm afraid."

"I don't know about that," Margaret said. "If you hadn't been wearing it you might have ended up like Nurse Kennedy."

"That's true. I hadn't thought of that. But what was it that you fired at, sergeant?"

"That I can't say, sir," the detective replied uneasily.

I was not prepared to let this go.

"Come, sergeant. You say you thought you saw something. What was it?"

"A figure, sir. I say a figure, not a person, sir, because that's how I saw it. A kind of outline. A whitish outline."

"Man or woman?"

"No way of knowing, sir. It was too dark."

"But what kind of clothes was it wearing?"

"No clothes, sir. It was . . . well, it appeared to be wrapped in bandages."

"Bandages!" I burst out. I could not believe my ears, but before I could question him further Margaret had interrupted.

"Sergeant, you say you shot twice at this figure you thought you saw!"

"That's right."

"Did you miss?"

"From that distance? No, it would have been almost impossible to miss from there. It was as close as I am to you now."

"In that case, what happened to the figure when you shot it?"

"That's what I can't understand, miss. The bullets seemed to go right through it as if there was nothing there."

TEN
The Claw Marks

There was a stunned silence as the three of us considered the implications of Sergeants Daw's words. In normal circumstances I would have ridiculed the idea. But these were not normal circumstances.

Suddenly the silence was broken as an irate Dr. Winchester burst into the room.

"So here you are. Sorting out your excuses, I suppose."

"No one needs an excuse, Dr. Winchester," Margaret answered icily. "At least, not in my opinion. I'm sure everyone did their duty as they saw it."

"Well, all I can say is I'm glad it wasn't me you were supposed to be protecting. I wouldn't relish the thought of waking up half hacked to death," the doctor snorted. "What happened up there?"

"Before we speak of that, Dr. Winchester," Margaret answered, thinly disguising her contempt for this outburst, "perhaps you would be so kind as to tell me how my father is progressing?"

This seemed to calm the doctor down a little.

"Of course," he said. "I'm sorry for not mentioning it immediately. His condition is stable again. Very much as before, in fact. Luckily I got to him before he lost too much blood."

"Thank goodness for that, at least. And Nurse Kennedy?"

"Another mystery, I'm afraid. No obvious injury, yet she remains in a trance, just as you saw her upstairs. I'm at a total loss to know how or why it happened."

By this time Sergeant Daw had recovered some of his composure.

"If you'll take a seat, sir, I'll try and fill you in on the details as we know them."

The doctor sat as Sergeant Daw explained what had happened to the three of us that night. The more incredible the story became the more fascinated the doctor was—and when he finally heard of the mysterious bandaged figure and the bullets that passed straight through it, his eyes positively glowed with excitement.

"Excellent," he said when the detective had finished. "Now we really are getting somewhere."

"For the life of me I can't see where, doctor," Sergeant Daw remarked. "I've no more idea what's going on in this house now than I had when I first walked through the front door."

"Oh, but you have, sergeant," Dr. Winchester insisted.

"How, sir?"

"Don't you see? At least we can now be sure who's not guilty of the crime."

"Can we? Who?"

"The man at the gate, of course. Jackson or whatever his name is."

Sergeant Daw shook his head. "We cannot be sure of that."

"Oh, really!" Dr. Winchester snapped. "The man is in your own police station. How could he possibly have been involved—unless he's got the power to spirit himself away without anyone noticing?"

"What if he has an accomplice who carried out the attack in order to try and divert suspicion from him?"

"Nonsense!" the doctor snorted. "Are you so stubborn that you are afraid to admit you made a mistake?"

"When I am certain that I made a mistake, sir," Sergeant Daw answered, as close to losing his temper as I had yet seen him, "I will be the first to admit it. Now if you stick to your profession, I shall try and stick to mine."

By now the two men were squaring up to each other, standing toe to toe as though they were about to fight. I threw myself between them and pushed them apart.

"Gentlemen," I said, "a little self-control, please. If we argue among ourselves we shall get nowhere at all. Dr. Winchester, is there anything new to report that might give Sergeant Daw a fresh clue to the mystery?"

The doctor was quite calm again, all trace of his anger having disappeared, apart from a reddening of the skin around his neck and a slightly moist brow. He thought very carefully before answering my question.

"Nothing new, exactly. Just a confirmation of something that I noticed yesterday."

"What's that?"

"The scratch marks around the wound. I think I must have mentioned them to you. Parallel scratch marks."

Here the detective began to take an interest again.

"Yes, sir," he said. "You did mention them. I remember quite clearly. In fact, I have it here in my notebook—'Unusual parallel scratch marks'—with a query: 'What caused these?' "

"Yes, well, I think I know what they are."

"What?" I urged.

"Claw marks!"

"Claw marks?" Margaret repeated. "You mean from some sort of wild animal?"

The doctor pursed his lips and shrugged his shoulders slightly.

"Perhaps wild—perhaps not—but very definitely crazed. Not only are there marks on the arm around the wounds, but the bandages that were ripped off were torn in just such a way as . . ."

The doctor came to a halt, not knowing whether to carry on with what he was saying or not.

"Go on, please, doctor," Margaret prompted gently. "In such a way as . . . ?"

Dr. Winchester looked down at his hands folded in front of him as though trying to avoid our eyes.

"As if," he began again, "as if a cat had done it."

"A cat!" I burst out, thinking how very ridiculous the idea was.

But then I realized what the other three had already remembered. Before the second attack, I myself had thought that I heard the mewing of a cat. A chill suddenly ran down my spine.

"Surely not," I said. "It's not possible, is it?"

"The only cat in the house is my Silvio," Margaret said. "He wouldn't hurt Father, I know it."

"No, of course not, miss," Sergeant Daw agreed. "But there's quite a bit of rough country around here. There could be cats gone wild. That wouldn't be unusual. I'll get my men to ask around tomorrow."

For some reason that I could not understand, this latest piece of information worried me, until suddenly I realized—my hand. I lifted it to examine the injury to my finger.

Dr. Winchester noticed the movement. "You have something wrong with your hand?"

"Oh, it's nothing," I replied. "Merely a scratch."

"Here—let me see."

The doctor grabbed hold of my hand and examined the marks closely.

"How did you get this?"

I looked at Margaret.

"It was an accident."

"How?"

"I frightened Margaret's cat—Silvio—he scratched me. He couldn't help it—it was my fault entirely."

"But these claw marks are exactly the same as those on Mr. Trelawney's wrist."

For a moment there was silence—then Sergeant Daw spoke.

"Are you certain about that?"

"Positive!"

Margaret looked devastated by this news—so much so that I felt I had to say something to calm her fears.

"Oh, really," I snorted. "This is ridiculous. Surely one cat scratch looks pretty much like any other."

"Yes, you may be right, sir," Sergeant Daw agreed.

But it was clear that Dr. Winchester was by no means convinced. And if the truth be known, neither was I—and it was with an even more troubled mind that I went back to bed that day in an attempt to catch up on the sleep I had lost the night before.

Strangely, though, when I woke again a little after nine that evening, I felt much more at ease.

I was to take the second nighttime shift with

Margaret, so on the stroke of ten the two of us entered the sickroom and took over from Sergeant Daw and Mrs. Grant. Margaret sat on the chair at the foot of the bed, while I sat behind her near the wall so that I had a clear view right across the room.

Mr. Trelawney lay on the bed, pale and rigid. The only sign of life was the regular rise and fall of his chest as he drew breath. His bandaged arm lay, as ever, on top of the bedclothes.

Dr. Winchester had agreed that there was something about the air in the room which encouraged drowsiness. He had therefore designed a kind of mask, similar to the one I had used the night before, but instead of a scarf and handkerchief, his were fashioned from pads of gauze and bandages. Each of us was given one of these to wear. We were also supplied with a small bottle of smelling salts which we could sniff at the first sign of inattention.

As a further safeguard we had worked out a system of checks between the two people sitting in the room. Every ten minutes I would walk over to the bed to see that Mr. Trelawney was safe and well. At the same time, I would signal to Margaret, who in turn would indicate that she too was in full control of her senses.

This system gave us both much more confidence that the night would pass without problems. And indeed for the first couple of hours it did. Time was passing much more quickly than on the previous watches, probably because every ten minutes I was able to stretch my legs and keep my circulation moving.

I could hear the clock in the corridor striking every quarter of an hour. Midnight came and went without any difficulties. Then a quarter past midnight. And then half past began to chime.

At this I stood up to make my ten minute check. But before I had taken more than a few steps toward the bed I was halted in my tracks by a sound that cut across the echo of the clock. Somewhere a cat was mewing. The sound I had heard the night before.

"Did you hear that?" I asked Margaret quietly.

There was no reply.

I glanced across. Mr. Trelawney lay on the bed, apparently untroubled. And at the foot of the bed Margaret sat as though she, too, was listening.

For a few seconds there was silence. Then from the far side of the room came a rustling sound. My heart was beating against my chest. It was happening again. I wondered whether to raise the alarm, but before I could make a move the mewing started once more. It seemed to be coming from outside the window. I stared in the direction of the sound. I could not be sure, but I thought I could see the outline of a cat.

I decided that the time had come to sort out this mysterious cat once and for all. Checking again that Mr. Trelawney and Margaret were still all right, I stepped forward, threw back the curtains, flicked the catch, and pulled open the window. As I did so a scratching, spitting ball of fur shot through the gap and knocked me to the ground.

Paroxysms of pain shot through my hands and arms as the crazed animal scratched and bit them. I screamed in terror and hit out to try and drive the beast away, but this seemed merely to incense it further. It changed the focus of its attack to my neck and face. Again and again its razor-sharp claws slashed into the skin of my cheeks.

I rolled over and over on the floor, trying to get away from the fiend, but it clung to me like a devil. Then, suddenly, the room was filled with light and I was being pulled to my feet by Sergeant Daw.

"What happened! What happened?" he shouted.

I looked around. There was no sign of the cat.

I put my hands to my face and felt the warm slipperiness of blood running down my cheeks and neck.

Sergeant Daw was shaking me now. Staring madly into my eyes and screaming at me.

"How did it happen? You must know!"

It was only then that I realized something else was wrong. I turned quickly to look at the bed. It was a mass of crumpled bedclothes. I switched my gaze a few feet to the side. There on the floor in front of the safe, his arm stretched out toward the lock and the bandages torn off to reveal his wounded wrist, lay Mr. Trelawney.

ELEVEN
The Detective's Suspicions

Margaret and Dr. Winchester were kneeling on either side of Mr. Trelawney. The doctor was working furiously to close the wound, which was bleeding again, although not nearly as badly as the previous night. As far as I could see, there was no fresh wound.

Margaret was leaning forward, staring fixedly into her father's face. Mrs. Grant was standing behind her. She took her mistress gently by the shoulder, but Margaret pulled away without shifting her gaze for one second.

Again Mrs. Grant reached down. This time Margaret twisted her head around and glared at her. Then, realizing who it was, her expression softened, and she allowed herself to be led away from her father and out of the room.

Sergeant Daw and I had been watching this incident without speaking, but as Mrs. Grant and Margaret left the room we looked at each other. He raised his eyebrows but said nothing. Instead, he handed me a large, white pocket handkerchief, which I gently dabbed against my face.

"You look a bit of a mess, sir, if you'll excuse me saying so."

I looked at the handkerchief. It was smeared with blood, as were my hands.

In the shock of seeing Mr. Trelawney attacked again, the pain of my wounds had been forgotten, but now the discomfort began to reappear. Sergeant Daw must have noticed, because he motioned me toward the door.

"I don't think we're needed here at the moment, Mr. Ross. Dr. Winchester can take care of matters. Let's see if we can clean those cuts and scratches up a bit."

He led me away from the sickroom and along the corridor to my bedroom. There he sat me on a chair before ringing the bell for a servant. Within a few moments one of the maids had brought a bowl of warm water, some iodine, cotton, and clean towels. The young girl looked long and hard at my face before going and could not resist questioning me about it.

"They say it was a demon that did that to you, sir. Is that so?"

"Who says?" I asked.

"In the servants' hall, sir. Was it a demon, sir?"

I tried to make light of it.

"No, of course not," I laughed. "How could it be a demon? There are no such things."

"What was it then, sir?" the girl persisted.

"I'm not certain. A cat, I think."

The maid shook her head slowly.

"No cat would do that, sir. No ordinary cat."

And without saying anything else—but not taking those wide-open, wondering eyes from my face for a second—she left the room.

The instant the door closed the sergeant rolled up his shirt sleeves and dipped the cotton into the bowl of water. He began with my face and neck, gently sponging the damaged skin with warm water.

"What did happen, then?" he asked, rinsing the cotton out in the bowl.

"As I said, a cat. I heard it mewing, just as I did before. It seemed to be coming from outside, so I opened the window . . . aaah! Be careful with that stuff!"

Sergeant Daw was now dabbing iodine onto the cuts to disinfect them. It stung as sharply as if a particularly angry bee had injected his poison into me.

"Better safe than sorry," he said. "Go on."

"There's nothing else," I said, flinching from the pain. "I opened the window and was hit by—well I'm not sure what. A cat of some kind. The next thing I knew, you were there."

"And Mr. Trelawney?"

"A mystery. Before I opened the window I looked across. He was there—in bed."

"And there was no one else in the room?"

"No, of course not. Except . . ."

"Miss Trelawney?" The sergeant suggested, turning his attentions to my hands and wrists.

"Yes."

"Why are you so uneasy about saying that?"

"I'm not," I insisted. "It's simply that . . . well, I don't want to give the impression that . . ."

Again my voice tailed off. I felt I was being drawn into a conversation I did not want to pursue. But Sergeant Daw was determined.

"The impression that she had something to do with it?"

I was feeling distinctly reluctant to discuss Margaret

in this way, yet I knew that Sergeant Daw would not let the subject drop.

"Yes, I suppose so."

"What did she do? While you were opening the window?"

"I can't be certain. I had my back to her."

"Did she say anything?"

"No, I . . ."

"Did she hear the cat?"

"I'm not sure."

"Didn't you ask her?"

"She didn't reply. She just sat there."

"Awake?"

"As far as I know. I couldn't see her face. It was turned away—toward her father."

I was beginning to feel as if I was being interrogated like a witness in the dock, the facts being dragged out of me one by one, building up a picture that threw more and more suspicion onto Margaret. I decided I had to call a halt before it went too far.

"Sergeant Daw," I snapped. "Are you trying to blame Miss Trelawney for what happened in there tonight?"

The sergeant had finished cleaning my wounds now and was drying his hands on one of the towels, carefully and precisely. He chose his words with equal care.

"I'm not blaming anyone, sir," he said. "It's not my job to blame. I'm simply trying to discover what happened. To do that, I have to ask questions."

"Yes, of course," I agreed reluctantly. "Please carry on."

"I think I've found out everything I want to know just at the moment, thank you, sir."

"In that case," I said, taking my courage in both hands, "will you answer a question of mine? When you entered the room tonight, what did you see?"

"I saw you writhing on the floor—clutching at your face."

"No cat?"

"No, sir."

"And Miss Trelawney?"

"She was kneeling by her father."

"Doing what?"

"She may have been trying to stop the flow of blood."

"Or?"

The sergeant hesitated before replying.

"Or, sir, she may have been trying to get the key to the safe off the bangle."

Part of me was astounded at the suggestion the detective was making about Margaret. But another part of me was less certain.

"You really think that Miss Trelawney may be connected with these attacks on her father?"

The sergeant walked over to the door and looked out into the corridor. When he was satisfied that there was no one there to overhear us, he returned, pulled up a chair close to mine, and, in a low voice intended for my ears only, answered, "Mr. Ross, don't get the wrong impression from what I am about to say. I've no proof one way or the other of what's been going on . . ."

"Yes, I understand that, sergeant."

"Then, sir, I'll carry on." He took a deep breath. "The point is this, you see, sir. There have now been three attacks on Mr. Trelawney. On none of those occasions has anyone broken into the house, as far as I can see. So reason tells me they must be carried out by someone already inside the house."

"One of the servants?" I suggested.

Sergeant Daw shook his head.

"No, sir. I was wrong on that score. Jackson will be released first thing tomorrow."

"Why have you changed your mind?"

The detective was uneasy.

"Well, I didn't say anything, sir, but tonight I kept watch on the corridor outside Mr. Trelawney's room. No one went into or out of that room once you and Miss Trelawney started your period of watch—not until I heard your shouts and entered myself."

"And to your mind that throws suspicion on to Miss Trelawney?"

"Miss Trelawney or you, sir," he replied. "But more on to the lady, I must admit, because on every occasion she has been involved."

"How do you mean?"

But I knew exactly what he meant, because the same thought had crossed my mind, though I was reluctant to admit it even to myself.

Carefully the detective spelled out his case.

"On the first occasion, no one else was present. We only have Miss Trelawney's word for what happened. At the moment I have no reason to doubt her word, but . . ."

"Go on," I said. "I'm listening."

"Very well. On the second occasion, you and Nurse Kennedy were in the room, it's true—but you were both overcome in some way."

"And the first person to get there was Miss Trelawney," I added. "And then tonight she was in the room again."

"Yes, sir," Sergeant Daw said, clearly pleased that I could follow his reasoning.

I was not at all happy, though. It seemed to me that I had helped to condemn Margaret when all I wanted to do was help her out of this horrible nightmare. I stood up and turned my back on the sergeant so that he would not see the misery in my eyes. Then I said, "So what do you intend to do now?"

Again the detective took me by surprise.

"Do, sir? Why, nothing. Just continue watching how things develop. There's no concrete evidence against Miss Trelawney, is there? Not that would stand up in court. No, at present this is nothing more than a theory—and not the only one, I might add."

But before Sergeant Daw could enlighten me further, the door to my bedroom burst open and Dr. Winchester entered.

"So this is where you are," he said, as though he had been looking for us everywhere.

"Yes, doctor," Sergeant Daw replied cheerfully. "We came here to clean up Mr. Ross's wounds."

The doctor had come straight over to me and was examining the marks on my face and neck.

"Yes, so I see," he said. "And a very good job you've done on them, too. You might have one or two scars there, though, I'm afraid. The same claw marks once again. How did you get them?"

"You saw nothing?" I asked.

He shook his head. "Just you writhing about on the floor. Nothing else."

* * *

The day dawned fine and warm. There had been a shower in the night that had freshened the plants and brought the world back to a sparkling cleanliness. Even those of us who had suffered so badly over the past few days felt cheered by the clear blue summer sky and the warm sunshine.

This was especially true of Nurse Kennedy, who returned to full consciousness during the course of the morning. To our great disappointment she could remember virtually nothing about the events that had thrown her into a trance.

Only Mr. Trelawney remained stubbornly unmoved by this glorious September day.

In the afternoon Margaret came to me and asked if I would be willing to accompany her on a visit to see Mr. Marvin, her father's lawyer. I naturally jumped at the chance to get away from the house for a little while.

I had seen Mr. Marvin several times around the law courts but had never been briefed by him and had never had cause to visit his offices, which proved to be as small and cluttered as I had expected.

He greeted us with great courtesy and showed considerable sympathy for Margaret and her plight. He inquired with genuine concern about the health of her father and asked how she was managing in the circumstances. But unfortunately, to our disappointment and his sorrow, he could add nothing to what we already knew.

"I can only stress," he said as we left him, "that your father was quite definite about what was to be done in such an event as this. He left with me the self-same instructions that are in his letter to you. He must remain in that room and nothing, absolutely nothing, must be removed from it. More than that I cannot tell you. Of course, if you need advice about money or the running of your father's affairs, I shall be only too

74

pleased to do what I can. Otherwise, I'm afraid I can be of little or no use."

Rather sadly we returned in the carriage to Kensington Palace Gardens. But when we got there, we were surprised to find that no one came to open the gate.

Again and again the groom rang the bell, but nothing happened. Finally Mrs. Grant arrived.

"I'm sorry, Miss Trelawney," she apologized, "but there's no one here to answer the gate besides myself, on account of the servants have all gone."

"Gone?" Margaret echoed. "What do you mean?"

"Left, miss—handed in their notice and gone without pay."

"But why?" Margaret asked, on the verge of tears.

"A lot of gossip if you ask me, miss, in the servants' hall. You know what they're like when they all get together. 'Strange goings-on.' That's what they said. Some nonsense about demons and not knowing when they'd be murdered in their beds, miss. I tried to stop them—told them they'd get no references if they went without giving enough notice, I did. But all they said was it's better to be alive with no references than dead with them."

As Margaret walked toward the house I could see that she was extremely upset by this new setback. There was no consoling her.

"What's worse," she said, "is that I can see just why they've acted in this way. How do we know that we won't all be murdered in our beds tonight?"

There was no real answer to this. It was a grim possibility that we had to face. But I did get one crumb of comfort from it. If Margaret was worried about her own safety, she could hardly be responsible for the attacks. So it was with some satisfaction that I went to bed in the late afternoon to sleep until four the next morning, when I was due to take my place in the sickroom.

In spite of my great fatigue, however, I did not sleep at all well. The cuts and scratches on my face, neck, and hands were sore, and for many hours I tossed and turned, unable to get any real rest.

Finally, some time after eleven o'clock, I fell into a deep, peaceful slumber that I think could have lasted for several days had it not been interrupted by a sudden outbreak of shouting and banging.

Afraid that another attack was being made on Mr. Trelawney, I jumped out of bed and sped along the corridor toward his room. Just before I reached it, the door opened and Dr. Winchester looked out.

"It must be coming from downstairs!" he cried.

We almost fell over each other to get down the two flights of stairs. In the hall the lights were fully ablaze, and for the first time we could see the cause of the disturbance.

Sergeant Daw was half-sitting, half-lying across a man I had never cast eyes on before. He had the stranger's arm pinned behind his back so that he could not move, though this did not stop him shouting blue murder as he struggled to escape.

As Dr. Winchester and I hurried down the last few steps to lend him our assistance, Sergeant Daw turned to us and in a triumphant voice called, "Gentlemen, I think we have him. We have caught our would-be assassin!"

TWELVE
The Intruder

As Dr. Winchester and I reached the foot of the stairs, the stranger noticed our approach.

"Thank God you're here," he shouted to us. "Get this lunatic off me, will you? He's completely out of his mind. He refuses to let go of me."

This took me totally by surprise and I hesitated, not knowing what to do. But Winchester jumped on top of the man with a whoop of delight and pushed his face down against the polished tiles of the floor.

"Hold him there!" Sergeant Daw panted.

Then, jumping clear himself, he pulled a pair of handcuffs from his pocket before pinning the man's arms together and snapping them on.

"All right, Doctor," he said. "Let's get him to his feet."

The two men took one arm each and pulled the intruder to a standing position. He was a short, sturdy, balding man, with tufts of red-brown hair sticking out over his ears. He had obviously spent a great deal of time in a hot climate, because his skin was as brown as a coffee berry and heavily wrinkled. His face was flushed and his eyes were burning with anger. He looked me up and down as though I was the one who had just broken into the house, and said, "What are you doing here?"

I had no idea how to respond to this and simply stood open-mouthed, trying to think of something to say.

"Never mind what we're doing here, my man," Dr. Winchester snapped back. "It's you that has no right to be here."

The stranger struggled to turn his head around far enough to glare at the doctor.

"I beg your pardon," he said in a withering tone, "but I have every right to be here. I am here to see the master of the house."

"Oh, yes?" Sergeant Daw butted in. "The master of the house? And who might that be?"

The stranger switched his glare to the other side.

"If you don't know that, sir, what are you doing here yourself? That's what I ask."

"I'm a policeman. That's what I'm doing here. And I intend to put you under arrest."

"Arrest? On what charge?"

"Breaking and entering for a start. And then later, perhaps, attempted murder."

The man swung his gaze slowly back to me.

"The man's an idiot," he said, shaking his head in wonder. "You seem to be the only half-sane person here. Will you kindly fetch Mr. Trelawney, so that he can instruct these idiots to unhand me. I know he is almost certainly busy at the moment, but tell him it is of the greatest importance. I have very urgent news for him."

I looked from the detective to the doctor, completely at a loss to know what to do. I had met a number of housebreakers during my career in the law courts, but never one like this.

The stranger dropped his chin on to his chest and

said sadly, "Don't tell me you're a fool, too. Is the house taken over by half-wits?"

Suddenly I found my tongue.

"I'm no half-wit, sir. And as for fetching Mr. Trelawney to see you, I only wish I could."

At these words the man looked up, horror in his eyes.

"What do you mean?" he said. "Is Mr. Trelawney in some difficulty?"

Dr. Winchester was becoming increasingly impatient with the course the conversation had been taking, and here he interrupted.

"Let's have no more of this," he snapped. "You know as well as we do that Mr. Trelawney is in no condition to leave his bed. Better, in fact—as it was you that attacked the poor man."

The stranger ignored this accusation and instead fixed me with his eyes.

"I implore you, tell me," he said. "Is Mr. Trelawney alive or dead?"

"Alive," I replied.

"Thank God for that," he exclaimed. "And in what state?"

"A coma, I'm afraid."

The stranger seemed to have forgotten his own plight now.

"I beg you," he said earnestly, "tell me everything you know about this."

By this time I think we were all having doubts about who was standing here in front of us—even Dr. Winchester.

"Who exactly are you?" he asked.

"A friend and colleague of Mr. Trelawney's, of course—here on urgent business. Now will you please remove these handcuffs from my wrist."

At this point Sergeant Daw decided to take control.

"I think there are a few more questions I need answers to before I can do that, sir."

"Really?" the stranger sneered. "And what are those, Officer?"

Sergeant Daw ignored the deliberately insulting title and carried on with questioning.

"Well, to begin with, how did you manage to get into the house?"

"With a key, of course."

"A key?" The detective was taken by surprise, and seemed at a loss for words. Luckily, Dr. Winchester came to his aid.

"Come now, do you really think we are so foolish as to believe that?"

"You need believe nothing," the stranger snapped. "Merely look on the floor to the right of the stairs. That is where my key is at this moment. It was knocked from my hand as I was jumped from behind."

I looked down. Sure enough, there on the floor lay a key. I stooped and picked it up. The key ring also carried a charm in the shape of a bright orange scarab beetle.

"That means nothing," Dr. Winchester said. "It could be stolen, or it could be a copy—taken by one of the servants, perhaps."

"It could be. But it isn't," the man responded icily. "It was given to me by Mr. Trelawney. Or perhaps you think he may have stolen it from himself?"

"There's no proof that Mr. Trelawney gave you that key until the gentleman himself recovers, sir. So in the meantime it's open to some doubt, if you'll forgive me saying so. Even if your story is true, it still leaves me wondering just how you managed to get into the grounds of the house."

"I would have thought that was obvious," the stranger sighed. "Even to a policeman. I climbed over the gate."

"Which proves you had no business to be here," Dr. Winchester snorted.

"On the contrary, it proves that there was no one there to open the gate. It seems that since my last visit the gate porter has either left Mr. Trelawney's employment or has taken to sleeping in the house all night."

"That's true," I found myself saying. "There is no one at the gate anymore."

Dr. Winchester glared at me.

"No, but there is a bell to ring." He almost snarled the words.

The stranger was ready for that.

"I did not want to disturb the whole household."

"Very considerate of you, I'm sure," the doctor sneered.

"Not considerate. It is just better that as few people as possible know of my visits here. That is why Mr. Trelawney gave me a key. That and . . ."

"That and what?" Sergeant Daw asked.

But the stranger's attention was no longer with the detective. Instead, he was staring up toward the top of the stairs as though he had suddenly seen a vision.

I whirled around. There, descending the staircase, was Margaret.

She was coming down slowly, one step at a time, her eyes fixed on the intruder. There was a strange eeriness about the way she walked, so silently and slowly—her eyes never faltering in their gaze for so much as a second. Even when she reached the bottom of the stairs she continued in the same way, completely ignoring us, the whole of her attention on the unknown man. Finally, she stopped just a few inches from the stranger, still staring deeply into his eyes.

He returned the gaze equally steadily.

Each seemed to be entirely absorbed by the presence of the other.

Then, quite suddenly, the spell was broken and Margaret spoke.

"Sergeant," she said. "This is the stranger I told you of. The one who came to visit my father so secretly some three months ago. This man is the answer to the mystery."

THIRTEEN
The Stranger Explained

It's hard to tell which of us was most surprised by Margaret's claim. For a moment we all stood open-mouthed, not knowing what to say. Finally I found my tongue.

"How can you know that? You told us you never saw him."

"No," Margaret answered. "But I did see his coat. And that," she said, pointing at the stranger, "is it!"

"Of course!" I exploded. "Why didn't we think of that?"

But Sergeant Daw was less excited.

"Not wanting to pour cold water on your explanation, miss, but the fact that the gentleman is wearing a similar coat is no proof at all. We need much more than that."

The stranger shifted his gaze from Margaret and fixed Sergeant Daw with a steely glare.

"You have more than that, sergeant. You have my word, too. I was here three months ago, although I regret that on that occasion I did not have the pleasure of meeting Miss Trelawney."

With a smile, he turned back to Margaret.

"It is Miss Trelawney, is it not?"

She nodded.

"I thought it must be," he said. "I have not seen you since you were three or four years old, yet I knew you the moment you appeared. I'm most terribly sorry to hear that your father is not well. Is there anything I can do?"

"The first thing you can do, sir," Margaret said, "is tell me who you are and what business you have with my father."

"Of course," the stranger readily agreed. "My name is Eugene Corbeck. I am Master of Arts and Doctor of Law at Cambridge and Doctor of Science and Oriental Languages at London University. By occupation I am an Egyptologist, and as such am the closest colleague of your dear father—and have been for the past twenty-five years. Now, if these gentlemen have no objection, I would be grateful if I could be given back my freedom."

Margaret questioned Sergeant Daw with her eyes.

He reluctantly took a key from an inside pocket and unlocked the handcuffs, releasing Corbeck's wrists. He folded the handcuffs carefully and replaced them in his side pocket. Then he returned the key to its place. Finally, when he could postpone it no longer, he cleared his throat and said awkwardly, "I think I must owe you an apology, Mr. Corbeck. I don't quite know what to say, expect that . . . well, you must see that under the circumstances it was perfectly natural for me to think that there was something unusual in your entering the house in this way, in the middle of the night. After all, not even Miss Trelawney herself knew you, and—"

Corbeck had been listening to this little speech with increasing irritation.

"For goodness sake, Officer, it was bad enough being jumped on and handcuffed without having to put up with you going on endlessly like this. You've no need to worry. I can assure you I have no intention of reporting you to your superiors—though I suspect I should, if only to make sure you don't go doing it again."

Sergeant Daw turned a deep scarlet, but Margaret stepped in and calmed them both with a few well-chosen words.

"I'm sure Sergeant Daw cannot be blamed for the mistake, Mr. Corbeck. Please, let us forget this unfortunate incident and concentrate on the matter at hand—my father's health."

This lecture had the effect of bringing us all back to reality with a bump, particularly Dr. Winchester, who was supposed to be on duty in the sickroom.

"Good grief!" he gasped. "Mr. Trelawney!" and dashed up the stairs two at a time with the rest of us close behind him.

As we approached the sickroom we slowed down, afraid of what we might find inside. But to our intense relief, the scene was quite unchanged. Margaret's father lay just as he had done for the past three days, looking neither alive or dead—in some state of suspended animation from which he might never be released.

Our relief, however, was not shared by Corbeck. Slowly he approached the bed, a look of horror on his face. Then he knelt down by the unmoving figure and reached over to touch his unbandaged wrist.

"How did this come about?"

As briefly as possible, Margaret related the happenings of the past few days. Corbeck listened intently, periodically nodding to indicate that he had grasped the point Margaret was making.

When she had finished, we all waited for his reaction, but he said nothing. Instead he made a tour of the room, checking the position of the various objects on the plan Margaret's father had left. Eventually, satisfied that everything was safely in position, he said, "All is as it should be. We knew that something like this might happen, even though we could not be sure what form it would take. But rest assured, my dear," here he spoke directly to Margaret, "your father has taken all the precautions necessary to come through this ordeal safely. You must place your trust in him. Now, I suggest we move elsewhere so that I can tell you my story."

"I think that would be a very good idea, sir," Sergeant Daw cut in. "Might I suggest the drawing-room, miss? And I think it would be best if Dr. Winchester and Nurse Kennedy could extend their duty for a little while tonight. It really is most important that you and Mr. Ross should hear what Mr. Corbeck has to tell us."

The nurse said nothing, simply indicating with a slight inclination of the head that she was willing and able to stay on. Dr. Winchester's reaction was quite different. He clearly resented being excluded from this important meeting, but as there was no one else to take his place he had no alternative but to agree reluctantly.

The four of us retired to the drawing room, leaving the doctor and nurse watching over Mr. Trelawney.

As we were seating ourselves Mrs. Grant appeared as if from nowhere, carrying a tray of tea and biscuits. Then Corbeck began his incredible story—the story that at last explained the events that were mystifying us.

FOURTEEN
The Story of the Mummy's Tomb

"The story begins," Corbeck said, once he was certain he had our full attention, "some twenty or so years ago. Trelawney and I were traveling in Egypt in search of treasures to bring back to Britain. It was our first major expedition, though we had both studied the history and civilization of ancient Egypt for some years.

"We had no particular route planned, but were taking advice as to likely sites from the leader of a group of bedouins who were acting as our bearers.

"One night, after a particularly trying day's march, we came to a narrow, steep-sided valley running east to west. The sun was low in the sky and I estimated that we had no more than two hours' light left before night fell. In view of this it seemed a good idea to journey part of the way through the valley and spend the night camped in the shelter of its walls. But when we suggested this to the leader of the bedouins he absolutely refused.

"'It is not a good place,' he kept repeating. 'No living creature can spend the night within its walls and be alive when the sun rises again.'

"We pressed the man to tell us why this should be

the case. But all he would say was, 'It is certain death to spend the night in the Valley of the Sorcerer.'

"'The Valley of the Sorcerer? Why is it called the Valley of the Sorcerer?' I asked.

"The man did not know for sure, but legend had it that long ago a king or queen who practiced magic had been buried there—and that the burial place was protected by a curse that brought death to anyone who went near it.

"Trelawney and I were struck by the genuine terror that the valley appeared to hold for the bearers—who by now had realized what we were discussing and were desperate to get away.

"Their fear simply made us more determined to enter the valley and see for ourselves whether there was any truth in the rumors. So, with roughly an hour and a half left to sundown, we persuaded the bedouins to set up camp some half-mile from the entrance and set off to explore the first part of the valley alone.

"The sheer cliff walls on either side were covered with carvings and inscriptions carved into the rock several thousand years before. As the sun began to sink toward the horizon, I heard Trelawney shout out in delight. Turning around, I saw that he was looking high up on the north cliff.

"There, some hundred and fifty feet up, was a circle of different colored stone. It was clearly manmade and in my opinion could be only one thing.

"'An entrance!' I gasped. 'It must be an entrance.'

"'But to what?' Trelawney wondered out loud.

"He did not have to wait long for an answer. I had already focused my telescope on the spot. What I saw there excited me beyond belief. Around the circle was an inscription carved into the stone. It said: 'Here lies the Nameless One. No gods bless this place, for she has insulted them and so must be forever alone. Go from here now so that their vengeance and her evil do not destroy you forever.'

"As I read this out my voice echoed back from the rocks. No matter how much we told ourselves that this was nothing but the superstitious mumbo-jumbo of a primitive people, we both felt a chill run down our spines. Neither of us wanted to remain near that place once it was dark, so we decided to come back the next morning and make an attempt to gain entrance to the tomb of the Nameless One.

"We set off early the next day with a team of four bearers to help us. They appeared to have no fear of the valley during the hours of daylight, and we knew that none of them would be able to read the inscription in the rock, so we thought everything would be well.

"We went through the valley until we reached a point where the cliffs were not so steep and it was possible to climb to the top without difficulty. On a spot directly above the tomb entrance the bearers set about fashioning a rope and timber cradle. This was to be let down over the side of the cliff with the two of us standing in it.

"A few minutes later, Trelawney and I were on our way down the rock face. As we reached the circular entrance to the tomb we found that it was nothing more than hardened clay, a couple of inches thick and sealed at the edges with a kind of primitive mortar. A few blows with a hammer, and we had made a hole big enough to crawl through. Seconds later we were inside.

"We found ourselves in a kind of entrance hall carved out of the rock. Leading from this was a passageway descending steeply into the mountainside.

We shouted up to the bearers to lower the lamps, and once they had done this, we set off on our journey, placing a light at regular intervals as we went.

"The tomb itself was one of the most magnificent I had ever seen. The workmanship that had produced the sculptures and paintings contained in it was breathtaking. And in that high, dry cavern, far away from the damp of the Nile, the colors of the artist's brushstrokes were as vivid and bright as the day they were first produced.

"This first part of the tomb was nothing more than an antechamber. From this, another short passageway led to a pit some seventy feet deep. This, we realized was the entrance to the burial chamber itself. Using ropes and hooks we made our descent. At the bottom, a tunnel led to the sarcophagus chamber, its entrance blocked by a huge stone door. To our surprise, it opened so easily and smoothly that we almost fell inside. The secrets of the burial chamber were revealed, and we could scarcely believe our eyes.

"The room was crammed with objects—most of which you have seen, for they are now here in this very house. The jackal-footed table carved from green bloodstone. The smaller alabaster table decorated with the figures of gods and signs of the zodiac. The turquoise casket with its lid that fits so closely we can find no way of opening it. And the magnificent mummified cat—all these objects and many more were there.

"But, without a doubt, the most striking presence in the chamber was the sarcophagus itself. It was made of a yellow-brown stone similar to Mexican onyx, with patches that were almost transparent. And it was huge—almost nine feet long and three feet wide—

every inch covered in exquisitely painted signs and symbols."

"The one in my father's room," Margaret exclaimed.

"And in my dream," I almost added, but decided against it.

"The lid of the sarcophagus was still firmly in place," Corbeck continued, "and there was no sign that the tomb had been broken into, so we knew that that mummy must still be inside the coffin. Our curiosity could not be controlled. We had to raise that lid, but we could not do it on our own. We needed help. While Trelawney remained in the burial chamber, I went back to the entrance to bring down more ropes and two of the bearers.

"There, in the depths of the mountainside, we set up ropes and pulleys above the sarcopagus, and inch by inch managed to lift the lid clear. We were not disappointed. Inside was the best preserved example of a mummy I had ever seen. The body—clearly a woman's—looked as though it had been wrapped only hours before. But it was not that which sent a chill down our spines.

"Across the chest—poking out from the bandaging —was an unwrapped hand. A hand with seven fingers.

"The flesh—it was undoubtedly flesh—looked almost like marble. Turned that way, no doubt, by the embalming that had taken place soon after death. I reached out and touched it. To my surprise, I found that it was still soft. I tried to turn it slightly, to examine the fingernails.

"As I did so there was a glint of red from within the fingers, which were curled over as though grasping something. Gently I pushed my own fingers inside the grip and felt something smooth and cold. One by one, I straightened the fingers. There in the palm of the hand lay an enormous ruby.

"Trying to hide my excitement, I took the ruby from the mummy's hand and slipped it into my pocket. I knew that if the bearers realized just how valuable an object we had found they might well decide to steal it from us. Perhaps even murder us in the process.

"For a little while we examined the inside of the sarcophagus, searching for any object that might be hidden around the mummy. But all the time our minds were on that blood-red ruby. Eventually, we decided to call a halt for the day. Trelawney turned to the bearers, who had been cowering uneasily in a corner of the chamber, and said, 'We will go first—you follow.' To our surprise the two men agreed.

"Trelawney and I made our way back to the entrance chamber, and then, after calling to those waiting for us above, up to the top of the cliff. It was some five minutes before the bearers in the tomb called to let us know that they, too, were ready to be pulled up. And then tragedy struck.

"As one of them reached the top, he missed his footing and plunged two hundred feet to the floor of the valley below. Looking over the edge we could see his body, spread-eagled, totally lifeless.

"Back at camp, we lost no time in retiring to the privacy of our tent to examine the ruby. It was even more magnificent than we had thought, both in its size and its color. Yet there was something even more unusual about it. Seemingly trapped inside it were seven marks—marks that looked for all the world like stars. Not only that, but the stars were in the shape of a constellation that can be seen in the night sky: the Big Dipper.

"Trelawney was particularly excited by this, as he had noticed the same pattern of stars repeated several times in the tomb. For a while we searched our minds to find some meaning for it, but then our musings were interrupted by a tremendous shouting and confusion of voices outside. I hid the jewel in one of my bags and we ran out of the tent.

"The bearers were gathered in a circle, talking excitedly. When they spoke in this way it was difficult to follow what they were saying, but eventually I realized that there had been another disaster. Two men had been sent to bury the bearer who had fallen to his death. While they were doing so they had been attacked by a lion, and one had been killed—the second bearer who had entered the tomb with us. Now both were dead.

"When I explained this to Trelawney he merely said, 'Well, at least no one else knows about the jewel now. Only the two of us.'

"Nevertheless, that night, before we went to sleep, I took the precaution of digging a hole inside our tent and burying the ruby in the ground. Then I placed my bed over the top of the hole so that no one could see where the sand had been disturbed.

"'Perhaps now I will be able to sleep soundly,' Trelawney smiled.

"And indeed for some hours we did sleep soundly, until just before dawn, when we were awakened by a hideous scream.

"We rushed outside, almost tripping over a body lying dead on the ground outside our tent. It was another of our bearers—the one who had earlier seen his companion eaten by the lion, we discovered later. He was lying face down. Being the first to reach him, we turned the body over.

"The sight that met our eyes chills me even now. He had a look of total terror on his face, his eyes wide and staring, his mouth gaping open, his lips blue. He had undoubtedly been strangled—his neck still bore the pressure marks of the hand that had done it. A hand with seven fingers—just like the hand we had seen earlier in the tomb!

"But there was a second, even more shattering, shock awaiting us. There, clasped in the bearer's deathly grip, was the mummy's hand itself. It had been hacked off at the wrist."

FIFTEEN
The Mystery of the Lamps

"The very sight of the mummy's hand there," Corbeck continued, "was almost enough to stop the heart, but a closer inspection held a further horror. The wrist was caked in blood—as though the three-thousand-year-old corpse had bled as a result of the injury."

Here I could contain myself no longer.

"No," I burst out. "It's not possible."

Corbeck looked me squarely in the eyes.

"That, young man, is exactly what we said. And we, too, were wrong."

I glanced around at the others. Sergeant Daw was watching Corbeck with a puzzled gaze, as though trying to decide whether or not he was speaking the truth. But Margaret had no such doubts. She was totally convinced by the tale Corbeck was telling.

"Please, Mr. Corbeck, carry on," she said. "How had the hand gotten there?"

"Oh, that was easy enough to work out. The bearers who had remained behind in the tomb had cut it off, thinking it would act as a magic charm. Probably the rascal who fell to his death was carrying it, and the others picked it up when they went to bury him."

"You think the latest victim was bringing it back to you, then?" I asked.

"Not at all," laughed Corbeck. "It's my belief he was coming to steal the jewel."

Here Margaret cut in.

"What did you do with the hand?"

"Buried it," Corbeck continued, "next to the jewel. Then tried to go back to sleep, but it was hopeless. Instead, we spent most of the night talking. We decided that, in view of what had happened, it would be best if we left the area as soon as we possibly could. First, however, we were determined to return to the tomb and remove all the objects that we could find there.

"We arose early—a little before dawn—as we had a busy day before us. The first thing I did was to move my bed and dig down for the hidden relics. Deeper and deeper into the sand I dug—and slowly I began to realize that something was horribly wrong. Both the hand and the jewel were gone. In some inexplicable way, the treasures had vanished. There was nothing we could do about it except pack our luggage and try to put the whole business out of our minds.

"So it was with heavy hearts that we entered the burial chamber that day. But, as Trelawney drew near to the sarcophagus, I heard him gasp with surprise. Not knowing what to expect, but fearing the worst, I stepped forward and held out my lamp so that the light was thrown onto the inside of the sarcophagus.

"There, on the blood-stained mummy's chest, lay the severed hand. And in the clutch of those seven deadly fingers was—the giant ruby!

"To say we were shocked by this turn of events is totally inadequate. Foolishly, I could only think we had been the victims of a trick. I turned around to look at the bearers who were standing in the doorway of the chamber, half expecting to see them grinning at us. But they seemed to be genuinely ignorant of what was going on.

"I decided it was best to keep it that way. Trying not to attract their attention, I reached in and turned the hand over so that the jewel was hidden from view before calling for the bearers to help put the sarcophagus lid back in position.

"After this, we spent the rest of the day systematically stripping the tomb of its contents. I supervised the removal of the objects, while Trelawney carefully copied as many of the inscriptions on the walls as he could. Well before nightfall we were on our way back to civilization—relieved to be leaving the Valley of the Sorcerer and the tomb of the Nameless One behind us."

Corbeck paused briefly, but then went on, "It took us three weeks' traveling to reach Cairo, and we had no particular problems on the journey. We had begun to think that we had left ill luck behind us in the valley. But we were wrong. A message was waiting for Trelawney that his wife—your mother," he said, addressing Margaret, "had died in childbirth. The baby—you!—was alive and healthy.

"The poor man was heartbroken. He immediately took the Orient Express back to England, while I made arrangements to bring the finds from the mummy's tomb back by sea. When I eventually arrived back, the funeral was long over and you had been sent to a nurse. Trelawney, though, had lost none of his sadness and despair. Still, the arrival of the objects from the tomb did seem to lighten his mood slightly. He threw himself into examining and studying them with single-minded determination.

" 'There is a secret locked away in these,' he said to me once. 'A secret that has been hidden for three thousand years. But I am going to discover what it is, Corbeck, mark my words.' "

"And did he discover what it was?" Sergeant Daw interrupted, suddenly taking an interest.

"Yes," Corbeck answered. "But not for many years. For two decades he spent every moment of his waking life trying to unravel the meaning of the many paintings and inscriptions we had found in the tomb. One by one he came to understand them—yet still an overall pattern could not be found. Until some eighteen months ago—I was in London working at the British Museum and staying in a room in Hart Street—I was awakened one night and asked to come straight here.

"Trelawney was waiting for me in the hallway. He was in a state of great excitement but would not tell me why, saying simply, 'All will be revealed in a few moments.'

"He led the way up to his room. A single candle was burning on his desk, and in its light I could see that he had drawn the jackal-legged table from the mummy's tomb over to a position near the window. Not only that, the coffin-shaped casket had been placed on top of the table in such a way that the two seemed to fit together exactly.

"What is it, Trelawney? What's going on?" I asked "Is it some sort of experiment?"

"You will see right away, Corbeck," he answered, "But first put out the candle. There must be no light in the room if this is to work."

"I snuffed the candle flame with my fingers, and Trelawney, who had moved over to the window, drew back the curtains. It was a clear, moonless night. And in the sky outside I could plainly see the seven stars that make up the Big Dipper.

"For a few moments we sat silently in the starlight. Then a strange thing happened. The casket began to glow, as though lit from inside by some mysterious power. At first I thought it was simply my imagination, but as the light became more intense there could be no doubt about it. I leaned forward to examine it more closely, but quite suddenly Trelawney closed the curtains, cutting off the light from the stars, and the casket began to fade again.

"'Now, Corbeck, what do you think of that?' he said, switching on the light. 'Do you know what caused it?'

"'Well,' I answered. 'I suppose it must have had something to do with the starlight.'

"'Exactly! Not any starlight, though—only the light that comes from the stars that make up the Big Dipper.'

"'Of course!' I exclaimed. 'The seven stars in the ruby. They are also in the shape of the Big Dipper.'

"'That's so,' Trelawney agreed. 'And that's not the only thing I've come to realize.'

"He went on to tell me that—knowing the burial chamber could never see light from the stars—he wondered if the casket would still glow if seven lights were set up in the same pattern as the Big Dipper. When he had tried this with candles it had worked, though not as well as with starlight.

"'So what do you think that means?' I asked him.

"'I cannot be sure,' he replied. 'But I have an idea

99

that somewhere in the tomb there must have been seven lamps that could be used for this purpose.'

"'No,' I said firmly. 'We left nothing behind. I'm sure of it.'

"'Then they must be hidden away,' Trelawney insisted. 'Perhaps in a secret chamber. You must go back, Corbeck, and find them.'"

"And did you go back?" Margaret asked, a sense of urgency giving an edge to her voice.

"Oh, yes, I went back." Corbeck nodded. "That's how I got this."

He held up his right arm to reveal his wrist. Right across it ran a deep, ugly scar.

"Good grief, Mr. Corbeck," I burst out. "How did that happen?"

"When I returned to the tomb," Corbeck began, "I found that indeed there was a secret compartment in the wall of the burial chamber. The door to it was opened by pressing on a particular sign. Unfortunately, whoever had designed this compartment had not wanted anyone else to remove its contents. As the spring was pressed and the door opened, a razor-sharp knife swung out from inside and struck anything that was in the way. I was lucky. It happened to be only my wrist."

"But what of the lamps?" Margaret asked, not giving Corbeck's safety a second thought.

Corbeck leaned back in his seat before answering.

"Gone! The tomb had been robbed. So I returned to England empty-handed. But not before I had contacted a number of dealers who I knew dealt in such relics of the tombs and asked them to keep a lookout for the lamps."

"But how did you know what they looked like?" I asked. "Surely there must be thousands of such lamps."

"Not thousands," Corbeck replied. "But a good number nevertheless. So it was there that I took a risk. You see, we had already found one lamp in the burial chamber, along with the other objects that had been left for the Queen's use in the afterlife. I guessed that the other lamps would be identical to that one, so I was able to show the dealers exactly what I was searching for."

"And have you heard anything yet?" Margaret asked urgently.

"Why, yes, my dear. Three months ago I had a letter from Egypt, from one of the men who was keeping an eye out for the lamps. He said he thought he had found them."

"Three months ago," said Sergeant Daw. "And that is when you came to see Mr. Trelawney."

"Exactly, sergeant. I received the letter while staying in Edinburgh. It took me a considerable time to journey here. That is why I arrived in the middle of the night. Trelawney was overjoyed. He had rather given up working on the project, but on hearing that the lamps had surfaced once again he returned to his studies with a vengeance. As there was no Orient Express due to leave for several days, I stayed on here and helped him before setting off to Egypt once more."

"And when you arrived there?" Margaret demanded breathlessly.

"I went to the dealer and bought the lamps."

"So they were the right ones?"

"Definitely."

"And where are they now?" Margaret's eyes were

fixed unflinchingly on Corbeck's face. Corbeck sighed deeply and shook his head in dismay.

"I wish I knew," he said, "I arrived back in Britain with them yesterday. I intended to come straight here, but when we landed in Dover, I was so tired that I decided to get a few hours' rest. I put the lamps in a wall safe in my hotel room. Locked the doors. Bolted the windows. And went to sleep. When I awoke they had gone—disappeared!"

"No!" Margaret burst out. "No, that cannot be so! Sergeant Daw, I beg of you, go now with Mr. Corbeck and see if you can find any clues in this matter of the lamps. I feel sure they must be connected with the troubles which have struck my father down."

The sergeant agreed immediately. The two men left for Dover within the hour, leaving Margaret and me curiously at a loss for what to do.

* * *

I spent the day sleeping, sitting with Mr. Trelawney, and walking in the grounds of the house. There was little to look at in the garden, but the weather was warm and sunny, and it felt good to be out in the fresh air.

Margaret slept for a while, too, and then busied herself around the house, as there were no servants apart from Mrs. Grant to do any of the chores. An attempt had been made to engage new staff, but word had gotten around that strange goings-on had been taking place at the Trelawney house, and no one wanted to work there.

As nightfall approached Dr. Winchester, who had been out visiting patients all day, returned. As he had not heard Corbeck's story of the previous night, he asked me to fill him in with the details.

I retold the events described by Corbeck as well as I could remember them, but the doctor was continually interrupting me for more information. He was totally gripped by the tale, and so desperate to discover the meaning of it that it was with some relief that I left him to begin my nighttime watch over Mr. Trelawney.

As I passed through the hallway on my way to the sickroom, Sergeant Daw and Mr. Corbeck returned from their trip to Dover. There was nothing but failure written on their faces. "A waste of time," Corbeck snapped. "Just as I said it would be."

Sergeant Daw was more thoughtful in his reply.

"I'm afraid there seems to be no real lead to follow up at the moment, Mr. Ross," he said. "I have left some men there to make inquiries."

"Inquiries!" snorted Corbeck. "They may make inquiries until the cows come home, but there are some things that cannot be explained away, sergeant."

I took my leave of them and made my way upstairs.

Mrs. Grant was to be my companion in the sickroom. She was already on her seat at the foot of the bed when I arrived. I picked up a mask from a side table and sat down in my usual place.

Trelawney lay as unchanging as the pyramids themselves. Every time I entered that room I looked for some alteration, some improvement in his condition. I never found it.

Already the routine of the night watch had taken over. While my mind wandered through my thoughts and fancies, I was still able to carry out the strict check procedure with Mrs. Grant. By now it had become second nature to me. As a method of ensuring Mr. Trelawney's safety it had yet to prove its effectiveness, but at least it made the time pass quickly.

I glanced at my watch. It was almost a quarter to one. I was so surprised by this that at first I did not take any notice of the noise outside in the corridor.

Then I heard it again—a door closing.

The unexpectedness of this brought me to my senses. It was not yet time for anyone else to take over from us.

Mrs. Grant had half turned in her seat, so I knew that she had heard it, too. I lifted my eyebrows. She nodded her agreement, so I stood up and made my way slowly toward the door.

As quietly as I could I opened it and looked out.

A figure was walking away from me along the corridor. I could not see the face, but I knew at once that it was Margaret.

Softly I called her name—there was neither reply or reaction.

Once more I called out.

"Margaret!"

A little louder this time, but still she showed no sign of having heard me.

Again I checked with Mrs. Grant.

She nodded.

I stepped out into the corridor and closed the door behind me.

A few quick paces and I caught up with Margaret. I reached out to touch her arm, but as I did so she stopped and turned toward a closed door. It was then that I realized what was wrong with her. She was walking in her sleep.

Slowly she reached out and opened the door.

It was pitch black in that room, yet she went straight to switch on the light as though she were awake.

In one corner of the room was a cupboard with a

drop-leaf front. Margaret took a key from a chain around her neck and unlocked it.

Inside was a set of seven Egyptian lamps.

I was completely at a loss for what to do. This was rapidly turning into a nightmare. Indeed, I was beginning to believe it could well be I that was asleep, not Margaret, when there was a shout from along the corridor.

It was Mrs. Grant, and there was a definite note of concern in her voice. In a panic I tried to get out of the room, but Margaret, who seemed to have heard nothing, was in my way.

As a result, it was some ten or fifteen seconds before I could get out of the room and back into the corridor. I raced toward the sickroom, not daring to think what fresh horror I would find there.

The door was half open and I rushed in. I was some way across the room before it hit me. Mrs. Grant was no longer in her seat. Worse than that—the bed was also empty. Trelawney's body had disappeared!

I stood dumbfounded, staring at the crumpled sheets. Then a steely voice rapped out behind me, "Stay right where you are. I am armed and will shoot to kill."

SIXTEEN
The Body Returns to Life

I stood frozen to the spot, not knowing what to do.

It was important that I make no sudden move that might push the gunman into firing. Also, I was aware that Sergeant Daw and Dr. Winchester could not fail to have heard Mrs. Grant's shouts, so at any moment they would be on hand to help—unless they had also been captured.

"Turn around. Very slowly," the voice snapped. "And be warned I shall not hesitate to shoot if it becomes necessary."

Slowly—very slowly—I turned.

There, not six feet away—with a revolver pointing directly at me—stood Trelawney!

A great shout of surprise and relief burst from my lips.

"Mr. Trelawney!" I cried. "It's you!"

"Who else could it be?" he replied, with no lessening of hostility in his voice. "This is my house."

The man clearly thought I was mad. He looked as though he might well decide to pull the trigger if I so much as took a deep breath, when Sergeant Daw appeared in the doorway.

Trelawney spotted him out of the corner of his eye, but his gaze and the direction of the gun never faltered. He kept it pointing directly at my chest.

"If you make one single move toward me, sir," he said to Sergeant Daw. "I shall shoot your colleague. Now who are the two of you? And what are you doing here?"

"Sergeant Daw, sir, of Scotland Yard. And this is Mr. Malcolm Ross."

For an instant Trelawney's eyes flickered toward Sergeant Daw.

"You expect me to believe that?"

The detective shrugged.

"If you're in any doubt, sir, I suggest you ask your daughter. She's coming along the corridor now."

Before Trelawney had time to react to this, Margaret had arrived in the doorway. For a second father and daughter stood looking at each other in silence. Then, with a cry of joy, Margaret was across the room and in her father's arms.

* * *

Half an hour later the six of us were sitting in the dining room downstairs. Although it was the middle of the night, Trelawney was tearing into a plate of cold meat, cheese, and pickles with all the appetite of one who had not eaten for four days.

As he ate, Margaret told the story of that terrible first night's attack. Gradually, as the tale unfolded, the rest of us joined in, adding what we knew. Finally we came to Corbeck and the disappearing lamps.

At that I leapt to my feet with a cry of excitement. In the confusion of Trelawney's recovery I had quite forgotten about them.

"Of course," I shouted. "The lamps!"

The others looked at me as though I had quite taken leave of my senses.

"The lamps," I repeated. "They are not stolen— they are upstairs!"

I raced upstairs and threw open the door of the small study. To my relief, in the corner cabinet the golden lamps still gleamed as brightly as ever.

With whoops of delight, Corbeck and Trelawney rushed forward like madmen. Sergeant Daw, Dr. Winchester, and Margaret simply stared at me, astounded.

After a few seconds, Sergeant Daw spoke.

"Mr. Ross, how did you know these were here?"

"Well . . ." I began uncertainly. I knew I had to take great care over what I said. The true story would undoubtedly throw suspicion on to Margaret, something I desperately wanted to avoid doing—at least until I had had a chance to talk it over with her.

"I heard a noise earlier on. That's why I left Mr. Trelawney's room. I thought someone had broken in."

Sergeant Daw was looking questioningly at me.

"I followed the direction of the sounds," I went on. "They led me to this room. I burst in, expecting to find an intruder. Instead I found this cupboard—open— with the lamps inside."

I felt certain that the detective did not believe me, but he said nothing. Then, quite unexpectedly, Margaret came to my aid.

"Yes," she said. "I heard noises, too."

I turned to look at her, totally dumbfounded. But there was not even a trace of deceit in her eyes. She totally believed that what she was saying was true. I was so shaken that I stood staring at her open-mouthed.

Sergeant Daw noticed my expression. He was about to speak when Trelawney, who had been talking excitedly with Corbeck while they examined the lamps, turned to us and said, "Very well, gentlemen. Thank you for your help, Now I think it would be a good idea if we got some sleep. You can find a hansom cab at the end of the road. Once again, my thanks for all you have done."

I don't know which one of us was most taken aback. After four days and nights of constant upset and worry, not to mention some little danger, we were being dismissed—sent home with a nod and a thank you.

Dr. Winchester attempted to put up a defense.

"Are you quite sure you'll be safe without us?" he said. "I, for one, would be much happier to spend the rest of the night here to make sure that everything is all right."

"No, no," Trelawney replied pleasantly. "That won't be necessary. Everything will be fine now. I'll be downstairs in fifteen minutes to say my good-byes to you."

Not knowing what else to do, the three of us returned to our rooms to collect our belongings together before gathering again in the hallway to wait for Trelawney to come down and see us off. He seemed to be in no rush to do so. It was twenty minutes or more before he, Margaret, and Corbeck eventually descended the stairs.

"Once again, gentlemen," he said, "my thanks."

He took the hand of each of us in turn and shook it warmly. As he grasped mine he leaned closer and in a low voice said, "Come again, tomorrow. Ten o'clock sharp. Then we will discuss what to do next."

Somewhat taken aback, I made the smallest movement of the head to indicate that I heard and understood.

The next thing I knew I was outside in the still, cold, night air.

* * *

"Kind of you to return so soon, Mr. Ross," Trelawney said the next morning as we took our seats in his study. "And you, too, Dr. Winchester," he added.

I had not expected to see Dr. Winchester there. And I have little doubt that he had not expected to see me, either. Still, we greeted each other without any sign of surprise, as though we really were the best of friends. Yet now more than ever I felt there were things I did not like about this doctor.

In the room, then, as Trelawney called the meeting to order, were myself, Dr. Winchester, Mr. Corbeck, Mr. Trelawney, and Margaret.

"Let us get straight to business," Trelawney said. "I have brought you all here this morning partly because I feel I owe you some sort of explanation for what you have been through in the past few days and partly because I need your help in the future."

"You have it, sir," Dr. Winchester exclaimed.

Trelawney surveyed him silently for a few moments before replying.

"Thank you. But before you make such promises it would be as well to find out what I need you to do."

He paused here as though considering where to start the story he had to tell. Then, with a nod of the head, he began.

"You need no reminding, I'm sure, that in the past few days a number of strange, we might say supernatural, events have taken place here—but none of you fully knows the reason for these happenings."

110

"Do you, Father?" asked Margaret sweetly.

"Yes, my child," Trelawney answered. "I think that now I finally do. Some three thousand years ago, in the land of Egypt, there was a queen—Queen Tera. In many ways she was not a good queen. She was more interested in magic than in ruling her people. She spent her life studying and perfecting this art so that she might attain power over all things.

"The priests did not like this. They thought that the mysteries of the world were their concern alone. They tried to turn the people against her, but the Queen's magic was too powerful for them, and she remained Queen until she died."

"Is that why they put her in that tomb—high up in the cliff—away from everything else?" Margaret asked, a look of real concern in her eyes.

"No," her father answered. "She chose the tomb herself—and not only the tomb, but also all the items that were to be buried with her."

"Why? What significance do they have?" Dr. Winchester interrupted.

"To explain that, I must go back to the time of her birth. Queen Tera was born at the seventh hour on the seventh day of the seventh month. At the exact moment of her birth a great meteorite fell from the skies. In the middle of this huge lump of rock was a jewel."

"The Jewel of Seven Stars?" Margaret asked in a hushed voice.

"Exactly," her father continued. "Seven stars in the same pattern of those of the Big Dipper—the very constellation that ruled her birth. More than this, the Queen had seven fingers on one hand and seven toes on one foot. Is it any surprise then that she believed herself to be in some way chosen? For many years she studied magic, trying to discover what it was that made her different from everyone else. Finally, she was convinced. She would not die—her spirit would leave her body only temporarily, and one day when conditions were right it would return."

"How?" Margaret's eyes gleamed at the thought. "How was this to happen?"

Trelawney was in full control now, as we each held on to his every word.

"In her tomb, she left everything needed to bring her spirit back to her body again. The jewel, the magic casket carved out of the meteorite that fell on the day of her birth, the jackal-legged table, and the seven lamps. She also left, on her sarcophagus itself, the instructions how these elements were to be used to make the magic work. How and when."

"When?" echoed Margaret.

"If my calculations are correct," answered Trelawney, "at midnight in seven days' time."

There was a deathly silence in the room as each of us considered the incredible implications of what we had been told. Eventually I could stand the silence no longer.

"You said you needed our help, sir. What is it you are proposing?"

"I am proposing, young man, that the five of us in this room carry out a great experiment: at midnight in seven days' time we attempt to give Queen Tera her wish and bring her back to life."

Again the stunned silence—this time broken by the doctor.

"Yes, but why us?" he asked.

"There must be seven people present."

Corbeck snapped into life. "We are only five."

But Trelawney had thought of this. "The Queen herself makes six. And her mummified cat in the corner there, seven."

"Her cat!" Dr. Winchester snorted.

"Surely you know, Dr. Winchester, that all great controllers of magic have their magical animals, too," said Margaret with a smile. "They are called familiars."

"Oh, yes. I believe I have heard something of the kind, now that you mention it," said Dr. Winchester, not wanting to look like a fool.

"So," said Trelawney, "are we all agreed?"

I felt I had to act quickly.

"Before answering that, sir, may I ask you just one question?"

"Of course, if it will help you make your decision."

"It will, sir. You see, as yet you have said nothing about the attacks that were made on you."

I saw Mr. Trelawney stiffen slightly. He clearly had not wanted the discussion to take this direction, but I knew that it was important I continue.

"Of course, sir," I said, "the attacks were made on you, and you have the legal right not to press charges against whoever was responsible for them. But Sergeant Daw will certainly wish to find out what happened. He has, after all, spent a great deal of time on the case."

"Daw is a fool," Trelawney burst out. "He would neither understand nor believe what happened even if he were told. He is entirely tied to what he would call the real world. The events that are happening here are totally beyond his mind. However," and here his tone softened slightly, "I understand your curiosity in the matter. And if you are to help, it is only right that you should be in full touch with the facts as I know them,

113

though I must warn you in advance I can be certain of almost nothing."

"That I understand, sir."

"Very well, then," Mr. Trelawney was less angry now, but his brow was still wrinkled as he began his story. "I had been working continuously for some thirty-six hours on my calculations of the exact time that the Queen had planned to return to her body, when finally I was overcome with tiredness and decided to sleep. I had just begun to doze off when I heard a noise. I tried to come to my senses, but was unable to overcome the drowsiness that had overtaken me. My mind was whirling around inside my head and I felt almost as if I had been drugged. The next thing I knew there was a hand touching my wrist. Not gripping, just gently exploring beneath the sleeve of my nightshirt. Searching for something.

"A whole series of things happened then in quick succession. There was a pain as something dug into my arm. I realized that the bangle on which I keep the key to my safe was being tugged, and the wire was sharply cutting into my flesh. Then there was a cry of anger. A woman's voice. Quite definitely a woman's voice and the screech of a cat. And suddenly a searing pain that shot through my wrist and up my arm.

"I tried to cry out for help, but no sound came. My arm was being thrown backward and forward, and I could feel claws or teeth, I wasn't sure which, repeatedly ripping into the flesh. I made one last effort to regain my senses, and for a second my eyes flicked open. I caught a glimpse of what I thought could have been a gown, an elaborately embroidered gown, before finally lapsing into unconsciousness. The rest you know."

It was a chilling story that left me feeling more uneasy than ever. I shook my head and said, "It's almost impossible to believe. Are you suggesting that it was the spirit of the Queen herself that did these things?"

"I am," Trelawney answered with no hesitation.

"But even if that was possible, why should she wish to harm you?"

Trelawney was suddenly nervous, the fingers of his right hand picking agitatedly at the bandaging around his left wrist.

"I am by no means certain she did mean to hurt me. It could be that she was simply desperate to get hold of the ruby from the safe. Without that her plans cannot succeed."

"So to get back her life she is prepared to destroy yours," I said.

Trelawney thought for a moment. "Yes, I believe she is," he answered finally.

"In that case," I said, "isn't it too dangerous to press ahead any further with this business? How many lives have already been lost since the day the Queen's tomb was discovered? Must others be added to that number?"

"Oh, this is nonsense!" Dr. Winchester butted in. "Don't you see? We are on the brink of a great discovery. The very mystery of life itself is what we are dealing with here. The secret is within our grasp. Of course it's not easy to understand, but we must go ahead. We have no alternative."

"I agree," said Corbeck. "There is an element of risk in all experiments. We have a duty to mankind to carry on now we have come so close."

"Two in favor, then," Trelawney said. Then, turning

to Margaret, he asked lovingly, "What about you, my child? I feel that much of the success of this venture rests with you. Will you join us?"

Margaret had been silent for some time. She was now sitting with her hands folded in her lap, her eyes lowered, quite calm.

"Father," she said, "I know that your whole life's work has led toward this point, and I would not do anything that might spoil the chance of its success."

Trelawney beamed with relief and stepped forward to take her hand, but Margaret had not finished.

"I also feel that I have been specially chosen to help in this task. That the Queen herself has picked me out. I cannot let her down. Whatever happens I must go through with it."

Trelawney folded his daughter in his arms for a few moments, then kissed her on the brow. When they separated again he turned to me.

"That just leaves one," he said solemnly. "Are you with us or against us?"

"With you," I heard myself say.

I knew that if I was to continue to be close to Margaret I had no choice but to go along with the experiment—yet deep within me there was a nagging, worrying, ever-growing doubt.

SEVENTEEN
The Underground Cavern

The great experiment was to take place in Cornwall, Trelawney explained. He had a house there that was well out of the way of prying eyes, particularly those of Sergeant Daw. The fact that the detective had been spotted keeping an eye on his London house made the move that much more important. Trelawney insisted that this was a matter of life and death, and he could not risk the police interfering.

One evening, Corbeck was sent out in the Trelawney carriage to lure Sergeant Daw away from the gates. Once the coast was clear, a second carriage conveyed Trelawney himself, Margaret, Dr. Winchester, and myself to Paddington Station. Behind us, two carts rumbled along piled high with crates and packing cases containing all the many objects from the Mummy's tomb.

"Have you brought everything?" I asked incredulously. "Even the sarcophagus?"

"Everything," Trelawney confirmed. "We must recreate the tomb exactly if the experiment is to work."

"And the jewel?"

"Here. Inside my coat."

I noticed, too, that Margaret had brought her cat

117

Silvio in a small wicker basket, which she placed by her seat.

I spent the long train journey sunk in thought, going over it all in my mind, still unable to believe it was really happening. After all, this was the nineteenth century, wasn't it? The Age of Science and Reason— not mumbo-jumbo.

At Westerton we left the train. Carts and horses were waiting to take us on to Trelawney House near Kyllian. It was, we found, a large, gray, stone mansion of the Jacobean period, vast and spacious. It stood miles from any other dwelling, on the verge of a cliff looking out over the angry sea smashing against the rocks.

Our first task was to unload the crates from the carts. That done, Trelawney paid off the men, and we were left alone. It was then that Trelawney sprang yet another surprise on us.

We were standing in the hallway, which was so cluttered with cases and boxes that it was almost impossible to move.

"Where do you intend putting all this?" Dr. Winchester asked.

Trelawney said nothing. Instead he took hold of the banister rails and pulled. The side of the staircase swung out, revealing a set of stone steps descending into the ground.

Margaret gave a squeal of delight.

"Well, I never," Dr. Winchester burst out. "Where do they lead to?"

"To an underground cavern," Trelawney replied. "Used many years ago by ancestors of mine who were not averse to a little smuggling."

"But presumably it is not smuggling you have in mind now."

118

"No, indeed," Trelawney confirmed. "Come with me and you will see for yourselves."

He lit a lamp that was hanging at the top of the staircase and led the way down the steps. At the bottom was a passageway roughly carved out of the rock, which ended in a heavy oak door.

Passing me the lamp, Trelawney took a key from his pocket, and with some difficulty managed to turn the rusty lock. As he pushed open the door I felt a slight salt breeze on my face and the flame of the lamp began to flicker.

Not knowing what to expect I followed Trelawney through the doorway. The instant I stepped inside I realized why we were there—this was to be the mummy's tomb.

A natural cave had been shaped in such a way that it resembled the burial chamber I had first seen in my dream. The walls had been painted with symbols and pictures similar to those on the sarcophagus, imitating exactly the Queen's final resting place.

"This is quite unbelievable," I said. "How long has it all taken?"

"Twenty years," Trelawney replied. "I began soon after I returned from Egypt. At first I had no real idea why I was doing it. It was simply a labor of love—an attempt to recreate Queen Tera's tomb here in Britain. But gradually I began to realize that I had to do it. That it was all part of the Queen's plan."

I looked around. Margaret was standing silently, staring at the paintings on the far wall. Once again she appeared to have slipped into that semi-trance I had noticed several times before.

"It's just as I remember it," she said dreamily. "To the last detail."

"Remember it?" asked Dr. Winchester. "You remember it?"

Margaret turned her head sharply. "Did I say remember it? I meant it is how I imagined it—from your description, Father, and Mr. Corbeck's."

We stayed on for a little while, examining the details of the wall paintings, but my mind could no longer concentrate on the matter in hand. I could think only of Margaret and her increasingly strange behavior.

We spent the rest of that day unpacking the crates and cases and carrying the objects down to the cavern below the house. By early evening everything but the sarcophagus and the mummy itself had been taken down. The sarcophagus we could not move until Corbeck arrived—even then it would be a very difficult operation. The mummy was not to be placed in position until the last possible moment.

As night fell we were all exhausted. After a light meal, I went directly to my bed and immediately fell asleep.

* * *

The following morning, when I went downstairs, I found Margaret sitting alone in the small, overgrown garden at the rear of the house.

"I knew you would come," she said softly as I touched her shoulder. "I've been thinking how kind you've been to me since I first met you. All the help during the time Father was ill—and now this."

"Really, it's nothing," I said. "It's the least I can do."

Margaret turned away again and stared out to sea.

"Whatever happens," she said, "I want you to know that I have enjoyed the time we have spent together."

"I was hoping that we would spend a great deal more time together in the future," I said nervously.

"I hope so, too," she answered. "But I fear it may not be possible."

"Not possible? Why not?"

"I'm not sure. It's just a feeling I have," she replied rather mysteriously.

She stood up and walked down toward the cliff edge. I followed her. There was a brisk breeze blowing in from the sea, and the gulls were soaring and swooping noisily above us. We stood side by side staring out across the endless expanse of water, neither of us saying a word. I looked across at her. There were tears on her cheeks. I caught hold of her and swung her around to face me.

"What is it?" I said. "What's the matter?"

"I wish it could be different," she answered. "I really do wish it could be different."

"What?"

"Everything. All of this. But it can't be."

"It can," I said. "Things can always be different. It's simply up to us to make them so."

"No," she replied. "Sometimes that's not possible. Sometimes we have to do things that we don't want to do, but that we are meant to do. We have no choice . . . I have no choice."

As she said this she kissed me lightly on the cheek, then turned and ran up the path to the house, disappearing inside the kitchen door.

I stood for some time trying to make sense of the things she had said, but without success. All I now knew was that I had to stop what we were doing before it was too late.

EIGHTEEN
The Final Preparations

Corbeck arrived the following afternoon. He was exhausted after a thirty-six-hour journey, during which he had caught a whole series of different trains and coaches in order to throw Sergeant Daw off his trail. He went immediately to his room and did not appear again that day.

I spent my time in the garden, looking out across the sea and trying to work out just what—if anything—I could do to stop this attempted reincarnation. Eventually, after much heart-searching, I decided that it would be best to make no move until the evening before the experiment was due to take place. At that point, I reasoned, everyone would be beginning to have their doubts. If they insisted on going ahead with the madness I still had time to telegraph Sergeant Daw and get his help.

Early the next day we began the process of moving the sarcophagus down into the cavern. It was not an easy business, and it was some three hours before it was finally in position and ready to receive the mummy.

At this point, Trelawney sprang yet another surprise on us.

"I have been giving the matter great thought," he began, "and as a result have had a change of mind."

For a moment my heart leapt with joy. I felt sure that

Trelawney had decided to call the experiment off, but his next words dashed my hopes to the ground.

"As you know, I originally believed that the mummy should not be placed in the sarcophagus until shortly before midnight tomorrow. I now realize that this is wrong. Not only that, but Dr. Winchester has pointed out that unless we first remove the linen wrappings that encase the body, the Queen may well suffocate when her spirit finally returns. He has therefore kindly offered to use his skill with the surgeon's knife to remove the bandages this morning."

"The sooner the better," Dr. Winchester nodded.

"Very well, then," Corbeck agreed. "Let us bring the Queen down immediately so that the doctor can begin."

While Dr. Winchester went to fetch his instruments, Trelawney, Corbeck, and myself carried the mummified body of the Queen down to the cavern. She still lay inside her wooden painted coffin, and it was not until we gently lifted off the lid that I had my first look at the mummy itself.

The outer bandages were in surprisingly good condition for their immense age—not nearly as frayed or dirty as I had imagined. But it was the severed hand that held my attention. It was lying on the chest a few inches from the end of the arm. The bandages beneath it were stained with blood, which contrasted sharply with the pearly white appearance of the flesh itself. It was a sight that seemed to have a grim fascination about it, and suddenly I began to understand the hold this ancient corpse had over Corbeck and Trelawney.

Margaret had gone to fetch more lamps so that there would be no shortage of light for the doctor to work in. We positioned them carefully around the body. Dr.

Winchester flexed his hands, chose a scalpel, and made the first cut.

The unraveling of the bandages was no easy task. Sometimes several layers were stuck together in wads with some kind of tarlike substance. At other times the linen crumbled away almost into dust under the doctor's fingers.

After a full hour and a half of painstaking work on the part of the doctor, it seemed that the wrappings were at last coming to an end.

"Almost there," he said. Then, in a puzzled tone, he added, "What's going on here? This is no bandage."

Dr. Winchester had started to remove a piece of linen from near the neck and found that instead of being only a couple of inches wide, it covered the whole length of the body.

"My goodness," Trelawney exclaimed. "Look at this, Corbeck!"

He put his lamp down and took hold of the other end of the fabric. Gently the two men lifted, and it came away from the body in one piece.

"What is it, Father?" Margaret enquired breathlessly.

"I'm not sure, my dear," her father replied. "I think it may be a robe of some kind."

Margaret held her lamp closer to get a better view. Then, with a cry of delight, she exclaimed, "It is, Father! It's a gown! A royal gown for the Queen to wear. And the condition—it's like new!"

Margaret took the gown from her father and held it in front of her. Even in the poor light of the cavern it was clearly a dress fit for a queen. It was of the finest woven silk, pure white, but delicately embroidered around the neck with tiny golden sprays of sycamore.

Similarly, around the hem there was more exquisite embroidery in the form of an endless line of lotus flowers.

We were all so excited by this discovery that none of us had noticed that beneath the robe still more treasures had been hidden. It was Dr. Winchester who first drew our attention to them. On the Queen's chest lay a wonderful necklace of gold and silver that glittered and gleamed with sparkling jewels of every kind.

The Queen's body was now fully revealed. It was perhaps the biggest surprise of all. There was none of the withering and dehydration that I had seen in the unwrapped mummies in the British Museum. The flesh was full and round, as in a living person, and the skin was as smooth as satin and the color of ivory.

But it was the face that took my breath away. Not because of its beauty—though beautiful it certainly was—but because of its likeness to Margaret.

My mind raced. I could barely believe this latest twist of fate. How could it be that two women, born three thousand years apart, could look so much alike? What did it mean? What forces were at work to bring this about? I knew only one thing—this dangerous dabbling in the unknown had to be stopped before it was too late.

"No!" I heard myself shout. "It cannot go on. It is foolishness to continue with the experiment. We must stop now."

As my voice echoed around and around the walls of the cavern, the others stared at me as though I had gone mad.

"Stop?" asked Trelawney incredulously. "We cannot stop now. Not now we are in sight of our goal."

"On the contrary," I insisted, "it is because we are

nearing the end that we must call a halt. You know how many people have died since you first discovered the mummy's tomb. It is the blood—the blood of the mummy's tomb. I tell you, there is evil at work here, and you are gripped by it. Who knows what tragedy lies in store if you try to go through with it?"

I looked around from one to the other: Trelawney, Corbeck, Dr. Winchester—and Margaret. My words meant nothing to them. No sign of understanding showed in their faces—just a grim determination to carry on with their plans.

Trelawney's words confirmed this.

"I take it then that we can no longer count on your help, Mr. Ross."

"My help?" I gasped. "I intend to do everything within my power to stop this insanity, if it's the last thing I do."

I turned and rushed from the cave. A few moments later I was back in my room with the door locked behind me. I had no time to waste. It was possible that they would take steps to prevent me leaving the house. I had to act quickly.

I gathered together my coat and hat, all the money I had brought with me, and an umbrella in case I needed to defend myself. It was not much, but it was all I had. Next I opened the window and looked out. If they were intending to stop me leaving they would already have mounted guard at the bottom of the stairs, but I still might escape down the sturdy cast-iron drainpipe running down the wall just a couple of feet away from the window. I reached up to pull myself on to the sill but was stopped by a knock on the bedroom door.

"Malcolm—are you there, Malcolm? May I come in? I'm quite alone."

It was Margaret.

What if she had changed her mind? If she wanted to come with me? Perhaps she was being forced to go ahead with the whole business against her will? Hadn't she almost said as much to me that day on the cliff top?

"Are you really on your own, Margaret?" I called out.

"Yes," she replied. "Please open the door. I must talk to you."

Not knowing whether I was doing right or wrong, I turned the key in the lock and pulled the door open.

Margaret stood, quite alone, in the corridor. She was looking perfectly at ease and—to my utter amazement —carrying a tray of food.

Seeing my surprise she smiled and explained, "The others are having lunch downstairs. I thought we might eat here in your room—it will give us a chance to talk things over."

She walked in and placed the tray on a small bedside table.

"It's all right," she said, looking at my coat and hat. "You don't need to go anywhere. I've spoken to Father. I told him that I was not willing to go through with the experiment, either. That it was too dangerous."

"And what did he say?" I asked, my heart in my mouth.

"He has agreed to call it off," she answered with a smile. "The mummy of Queen Tera will never be brought back to life."

I was so overjoyed that I threw my arms around Margaret and hugged her to me. When I released her she was blushing heavily and slightly breathless. For a moment neither of us knew what to say, then, kneeling down by the table, she began to pour the tea from a pot into two china cups.

"Would you like a sandwich?" she asked. "They're only cold beef, I'm afraid."

"Not at the moment. I'm not hungry. I'll just have tea—hot sweet tea. They say it's good for shock."

"Exactly what Dr. Winchester prescribed." She laughed and passed me a cup.

I took a drink. The tea was very sweet but I gulped it down eagerly. I had so much to say to Margaret that I didn't know where to start. I reached down and took her hand. It was suddenly hot and stuffy in the room, and I thought we would be better sitting near the open window.

I started to tell her what I had intended to do, but my tongue refused to say the words. Instead I could hear a kind of slurred gabbling that made no sense to me.

My head was spinning now, and I could barely see Margaret's face looking up at me. I reached out to steady myself and heard the cup and saucer crash to the floor. Too late I realized what had happened. The tea had been drugged.

It was my final thought before I was enveloped in darkness.

NINETEEN
The Mummy Comes to Life

I opened my eyes. The room was black and silent. I was lying on the bed. I turned slowly on to my side and tried to sit up. Immediately my head began to thump and I felt violently sick. I slumped back against the mattress.

I waited until the noise inside my skull had died down and tried again. This time I managed to swing myself into a sitting position on the side of the bed. My insides were heaving, and once more I had to stay quite still for some minutes until the sensation had passed.

During this time I listened carefully. There was not a sound from any part of the house. Everyone must be asleep.

I was still fully dressed. I reached into my pocket and brought out my watch. I peered down at it but it was hopelessly dark. I couldn't even begin to make out the position of the fingers. Just then the room brightened as a shaft of moonlight shone in through the window, the curtains being wide open. Turning, I held the watch in a pool of light. It was half past eleven.

Desperately I tried to gather my thoughts together, and slowly the events of the previous day came back to me. I had been drugged—that much was clear—to stop me leaving the house. Obviously, though, I had awakened earlier than they had expected.

My heart leapt. I still had a chance to escape and contact Sergeant Daw. But I had to move immediately while they were all asleep and before anyone realized that I was no longer incapacitated.

I took a deep breath and tried to push myself forward on to my feet. For a few seconds I swayed from side to side, fighting to keep my balance—my senses were whirling—then suddenly my head cleared and I felt in control again.

I glanced around the room. My belongings had gone—I was left with nothing but the clothes I stood up in. Still, time was on my side. I might have several hours before anyone discovered that I was gone, and by that time I would have reached the nearest village.

With no great hope I walked to the door, and to my great surprise it was unlocked. I could hardly believe my luck. Clearly they had been so confident that I would not wake up that they had not bothered to take the simple precaution of locking the door.

I stepped out.

At that instant the house was suddenly filled with an earsplitting, unearthly yowling that made my blood run cold.

A few steps along the corridor and I was at the top of the stairwell. The noise was much louder there and was accompanied by frantic scrabbling and scratching sounds.

I realized what it was—Silvio, Margaret's cat. He appeared to be attacking something in the hallway below. Encouraged, I made my way rapidly downstairs. Near the bottom I stopped. I could see the cat now—he was in a half-crazed state, hurling himself against the wooden paneling that made up the side of the stairs, scratching and biting as though trying to rip his way through.

Still there had been no response from anyone else in the house. It was impossible to believe that the noise had not been heard—it was enough to wake the dead.

To wake the dead!

Of course!

All at once my thoughts crystallized and I knew what was happening. I had been unconscious not for twelve hours, as I had assumed, but for thirty-six hours—a day and a half. That explained why no one was coming to investigate Silvio's rantings. Everyone was down in the cavern, preparing for the experiment.

I examined my watch. Twenty to twelve. I had just twenty minutes to find a way of stopping the great experiment.

I grabbed hold of the banister rails and swung the side of the staircase out to reveal the secret steps. I went down these two and three at a time, but even so I arrived at the oak door well behind Silvio, who was already attacking the wood with his claws.

I grasped the handle and tried to push the door open, but it was firmly locked. I stepped back three paces and hurled myself against it. My shoulder hammered into the rough planking but it did not give in the slightest degree. I knew then that it was hopeless—that door could never be broken down by one man.

In despair I hammered on it with my fists and shouted at the top of my voice, "Margaret! Margaret—don't do it! Come out!"

There was no reply.

Then I remembered the very first time Trelawney had taken us to that cavern. As he had opened the door there had been a distinct breeze and the smell of salt. That could mean only one thing—somewhere there had to be another entrance to the cave, from the cliff top or from the beach.

Yes, the beach—it had to be the beach. Hadn't Trelawney said that his ancestors had used the cave for smuggling? There had to be a way in from the beach.

I raced back up the stone steps and out of the house. A little way along the cliff I knew there was a path that went down to the sea. Minutes later I was stumbling along the rough ground, my eyes searching the cliffs for the entrance to a cave.

My heart sank. As far as I could see there was no opening of any kind in the rock face. Perhaps I was wrong—perhaps the entrance was from the top of the cliffs after all.

I had just decided to turn back and retrace my steps when I noticed moonlight glinting on water. A stream ran from the base of the cliffs down into the sea. Could that be the entrance I was looking for?

I quickened my pace and made directly for the source of the stream. As I got nearer my spirits soared. Where the bubbling stream emerged from the rocks there was an opening just big enough for a man to squeeze through.

I had no time to stop and think. This was my only chance. If my idea was wrong, then all was lost.

I squeezed through the gap. To my relief, it opened out into a much larger cave. It was pitch black in there. I could see nothing and had to feel my way along the wall as I stumbled forward. The passageway seemed to lead upward at a considerable angle.

For some minutes I pressed on, still unsure of whether or not I was on the right track. Then my nostrils caught the scent that told me I was: the unmistakable smell of tar and spices—the smell of the mummy's tomb.

Encouraged by this, I tried to increase my speed, but it was hopeless. Not only could I still not see my hand in front of my face, but also the roof of the passageway seemed to be getting lower. Several times I banged my head, and by the time I had gone another thirty or forty yards I was bent almost double.

Still I carried on, determined not to give up, but I knew that time was not on my side. I could not see my watch, but I felt certain that it could not be more than five minutes to the magic hour of midnight. By this time I was crawling on my hands and knees and was beginning to fear that the passage would soon come to a dead end. Then, twenty yards ahead, I saw a patch of light.

I scrabbled onward, but almost immediately found I could go no further. Some kind of landslide had partly blocked the tunnel, and there was no way through. In a mad panic I tore at the loose rocks with my bare hands, trying to clear a big enough gap to allow me to squeeze through.

Eventually I had done it and was able to continue my progress toward what I could now see was an opening in the floor. Light was filtering up from beneath, and I could hear a noise—a low-pitched hum, coming and going but growing stronger each time it returned— just as I had heard in my dream.

The great experiment had started.

On all fours I scrambled the last few yards to the point where I could look down into the cave. I thrust my face forward into the gap. For a moment I could see nothing, my eyes blinded by the light from below.

Slowly, as my sight adjusted, I began to be able to make out the scene. Four figures were gathered around the sarcophagus and staring down at the body of the Queen: Margaret and her father at either side, Corbeck and Dr. Winchester at the foot. The jackal-legged table had been placed at the head, and on top of it lay the magic casket.

Along the far wall the seven lamps were positioned in the by now familiar pattern of the Big Dipper. They were burning with an intense glare that filled the chamber with a harsh white light, casting long, eerie shadows and giving the whole scene an unearthly, otherworld appearance.

Inside the sarcophagus at the mummy's feet I could see the folded silk gown and necklace that had been wrapped inside her bandages. Also a plate of fresh fruit, a goblet of water, and a bouquet of flowers. The preparations for her rebirth had been thorough.

By now the oil in the lamps had burned itself out. One by one they began to flicker and die, yet the tomb did not fall into darkness. The casket at the head of the sarcophagus was beginning to glow with an inner light. At first it was nothing more than a slight enhancement of its natural coloring, but gradually the light grew and grew till it glowed like a blazing jewel.

But this was not the only source of illumination, as I now saw. The massive ruby—the Jewel of Seven Stars—had been replaced in the palm of the mummy's severed hand and was now throwing out a piercing beam of blood-red light.

There was a tiny muffled explosion, and I saw that the lid of the casket had lifted a few inches and was hovering in mid-air. Smoke was beginning to steal out from it, thick white smoke rolling over the sarcophagus and surrounding the four standing figures so that it looked as if they were somehow floating on clouds.

Suddenly I was overcome with fear. I found myself screaming down into the cave, "Margaret! Get out, Margaret, before it's too late!"

But my cries were completely drowned out by the humming sound that had gradually been increasing in pitch so that now it was a piercing, mind-numbing shriek.

Still the smoke poured out from the casket, but its color was changing. First to pink, then red, then a deep rich crimson the color of blood. Unfurling over the sides of the sarcophagus, it gave the appearance of bathing the mummy in that life-giving liquid without which no body could stay alive.

At the same time the sarcophagus had started to pulsate, like a beating human heart, so that the cave was filled with a regular pulsing noise like the sound of blood coursing through arteries. Gradually the surroundings began to pick up this rhythmic motion, so that the whole of the hillside appeared to be beating in tune to the force emanating from the sarcophagus.

By this time the smoke below was so dense that I had almost lost sight of the mummy and the four figures surrounding it, catching only brief glimpses at irregular intervals. Still the pulsing continued. I could feel the regular waves passing through the rocks surrounding me, like an earthquake—so much so that I began to fear for my safety. Surely it was only a matter of time before the tunnel caved in, burying me forever.

Again I screamed down into the cave, "Margaret! Get out, Margaret! For my sake get out now!"

But it was hopeless. The noise was enormous. No voice could possibly be heard through it.

I had to get out. Already, bits of rock were breaking off from the roof of the tunnel and clattering down around me. If I left it any longer I knew I would never escape. I took one last look down into the smoke-filled cave. I could see nothing—not even the dimmest outline of the sarcophagus or the figures that had surrounded it. Then, suddenly, there was an ear-splitting scream of triumph and an explosion of light, and for a moment the scene was as clear as daylight.

The sarcophagus was empty. The mummy had gone, but at its side was a living, radiant figure in a flowing white silk robe, the Queen's magnificent necklace sparkling around her throat. It was Margaret. For an instant she looked up toward me and then, as quickly as it had come, the light disappeared and I could see nothing.

The rocks around me were creaking and sliding, and dust was filling my eyes and mouth. It was now or never—I had to get out. I scrambled backward along the tunnel as fast as I could go, but I knew that it was hopeless. The walls of the cave were shuddering and likely to collapse at any moment. Then, from the secret cavern, there came an enormous roaring explosion and I was engulfed in a mass of falling debris.

I heard myself cry out in pain, and then I knew no more.

* * *

It was daylight.

And I was on the seashore, looking up into a dazzling blue sky. I had no idea how I had gotten there, but I was alive.

A voice spoke. "Take it easy, sir. Just lie quiet for a while—you've had a rough time."

I twisted my head in the direction of the sound and a

face swam into view. It was Sergeant Daw. He smiled down at me.

"Thought you'd had it, when we pulled you out from under them rocks, sir."

My mouth was parched and gritty with dust.

"Have you got any water?" I asked.

The sergeant reached down under my shoulders and helped me into a half-sitting position before putting a flask to my lips. I took a deep drink of cool, sweet water, rinsed it around my mouth, and swallowed. Then I struggled forward so that I could rest my head on my knees, and as I did so my thoughts snapped into focus.

"Margaret," I exclaimed. "What happened to Margaret?"

Sergeant Daw shrugged his shoulders sadly and nodded for me to look behind me.

The sight that met my eyes was a scene of total destruction. A large section of the top of the cliff had slid forward and crashed down on to the beach below, undermining the front wall of the house, which had in turn collapsed, bringing the roof down with it.

"Nobody could live through that, sir," the sergeant said softly.

There were tears in my eyes, and I was forced to look away.

"I should have stopped them," I said. "I should have found a way to stop them."

"You tried, sir," the detective replied. "We all tried—but there was something driving them on. I don't know what it was."

"I think I do," I answered. "Or at least who it was."

"Yes, well, it's over now, sir. You just rest here quietly. I've got two of my men coming back here with a doctor to check you over before we try moving you. Don't want to take any more chances."

The sergeant stood up and took a few paces toward the sea; then, as though he had suddenly remembered something, he turned and came back. Reaching down into his jacket pocket, he removed an object that he had wrapped in a white handkerchief and crouched down to show it to me.

"By the way, sir, do you know what this is? The local police found it earlier when we were searching the beach."

Carefully he unfolded the handkerchief. There, in the palm of his hand, was the mummy's necklace.

I reached across and took it from him. In the sunlight the gems still sparkled as brightly as ever, but on the golden clasp that fastened the two ends together there was a single drop of congealed blood.

For a moment I was lost in thought. Sergeant Daw's voice brought me back to the present.

"Do you know what it is, sir?"

"Oh, yes, sergeant," I answered. "I know what it is. That is blood. Blood from the mummy's tomb."